Just some of the [...]
Lauren La [...]

'A powerhouse romance author'
PopSugar

'A delight – as sweet and bubbly as a glass of champagne'
Beth O'Leary, *Sunday Times* bestselling author

'The word charm is pretty much synonymous with Lauren Layne'
Hypable

'The queen of contemporary New York City romance'
BookPage (starred review)

'She's the queen of witty dialogue!'
Rachel Van Dyken, *New York Times* bestselling author

'Lauren Layne's books are as effervescent and delicious as a brunch
mimosa. As soon as you read one, you're going to want
another – IMMEDIATELY!'
Karen Hawkins, *New York Times* bestselling author

'Sweet and full of humor . . . readers will be
rooting for Gracie to find her Prince Charming'
Booklist

'Layne crafts a gleefully shameless homage
to *Little Shop Around the Corner* and *You've Got Mail* that
sparkles like champagne fizz . . . A delight'
Publishers Weekly (starred review)

'A charming, swoony, funny, must-read delight of a book!'
Evie Dunmore, *USA Today* bestselling author

'The perfect read while sipping a mai tai on the sand' *Cosmopolitan*

By Lauren Layne

Standalones
The Prenup
To Sir, With Love
Made In Manhattan
You, Again

Wedding Belles Series
From This Day Forward (e-novella)
To Have And To Hold
For Better Or Worse
To Love And To Cherish

Oxford Series
Irresistibly Yours
I Wish You Were Mine
Someone Like You
I Knew You Were Trouble
I Think I Love You

Love Unexpectedly Series
Blurred Lines
Good Girl
Love Story
Walk Of Shame
An Ex For Christmas

I Do, I Don't Series
Ready To Run
Runaway Groom

The Central Park Pact Series
Passion On Park Avenue
Love On Lexington Avenue
Marriage On Madison Avenue

You, Again

LAUREN LAYNE

HEADLINE
ETERNAL

First published in Great Britain in 2022
by HEADLINE ETERNAL
An imprint of HEADLINE PUBLISHING GROUP

1

Cataloguing in Publication Data is available from the British Library

ISBN 978 1 4722 9364 0

Typeset in 11.55/16.25 pt Granjon LT Std by Jouve (UK), Milton Keynes

Printed and bound in Great Britain by Clays Ltd, Elcograf S.p.A.

HEADLINE PUBLISHING GROUP
An Hachette UK Company
Carmelite House
50 Victoria Embankment
London EC4Y 0DZ

www.headlineeternal.com
www.headline.co.uk
www.hachette.co.uk

You, Again

CHAPTER ONE

Friday, September 9

⌢

"*A*nother Malbec?"

I glance up from my phone at the bartender, and the fact that she already has the wine bottle poised over my glass makes me think I'm not doing a great job of hiding the fact that I've just been stood up.

I smile and nod in thanks as she tops my glass off rather generously, then turn my attention back to my phone.

God bless Collette. My best friend has maintained a reassuring, steady barrage of messages, all of the *men can rot* variety.

Indeed.

But whereas my best friend is blowing up my phone in grand style, my date, on the other hand, remains steadily, painfully silent.

I suck in my cheeks, and for the tenth time, debate the possibility of texting *him*. Just something cute and nonchalant. *Hey, did we cross wires? Hey, am I at the right place? Hey, did I get the wrong date?*

If I tack a casual *lol* on the end of it. That erases any note of vulnerability, right?

Haha, whoops, did my assistant put the wrong date in my calendar, lol.

There! I start to type. That's downright *breezy*.

With a little groan of disgust, I delete the message without hitting send. I don't even have an assistant.

I take a sip of wine and say a regretful goodbye to the opportunity to explore Kris Powers' intriguing tattoos up close and personal tonight. I suppose that's what I get for crushing on a trainer at my gym. If I've learned anything from my flaky, free-spirited mother, it's to never pursue a man who's better-looking than you.

But *oh*, how I like the pretty bad boys.

Give me a guy with too-long hair, an aversion to razors, and an inked-up, sculpted bicep, and I end up, well . . . *here*. Nursing wine, alone, because I've got a soft spot for men I can't count on.

Like mother, like daughter . . .

It's the way of us Austin ladies. The "settle down" gene skipped right on by us. In place of the commitment chromosome, we got what I like to think is a charming blend of wild child and free spirit.

I mean, we're not *feral*. It's just that our romantic philosophy leans towards love the one you're with, and *love* translates more to, well, *sex*.

But I'm not a cynic. Really, I'm not. I believe in happily-ever-after! I just don't happen to believe that happily-ever-after has to involve a man—or at least not be limited to *one* man.

Which is why my below-the-waist parts are disappointed at

Kris's no-show, but there will be no mourning beyond a brief case of Lady Blue Balls.

There are, after all, always other fish in the sea.

And in Manhattan? There are a whole lotta fish. And I know just where to find them: TapThat.

As in, my favorite dating app of late.

Yeah, yeah. I know. Classy.

But also? Sort of addicting.

TapThat happily exploits our human proclivity for snap decisions and gut reactions. You're presented with a potential match, and then you get five seconds and *only* five seconds to decide whether you're feeling it.

Double tap for *hell yeah*, or do nothing and the guy fades away.

Is it the most cerebral and thoughtful of dating apps? Nah. In fact, it's quickly developed a reputation as the hookup app more than the meet-your-future-spouse app, but as we've established, that suits me *just fine*.

Especially on nights like tonight when I have no intention of letting my cute, lacy thong go unseen all because of a flaky gym rat.

I open the app, thumb at the ready. I know within a half second that the first match is a no. The guy is probably sweet, but I'm definitely not into the bright coral bow tie.

The second guy warrants two seconds of deliberation—the body's an A-plus, but the purposeful way he's leaning against a shiny red car gives me the sense he knows more about how Porsche's parts work than *my* parts, if you get what I'm saying.

I let him fade away.

A third comes up and he's an *immediate* double tap. *Oh mama.*

But he's also a long shot. He looks like a young Idris Elba, and I'm like, a 6.5 on a really good day.

I'll need a backup plan, so I move onto Guy #4, who's an *eventual* yes, earning a double tap just as his image starts to fade away. I'm a sucker for hair falling out of a man bun, but my loins aren't exactly throbbing at the popped collar of his baby blue polo.

One more, just to build my safety net.

Guy #5 is . . . *hmm*.

The eyes are amazing, I'll give him that. That sort of muted pale blue that looks almost gray. But he's also *super* intense, and his unimaginative haircut and gray suit have him looking a bit like a stock photo for "successful businessman."

My thumb stays still without tapping, and I let him fade into obscurity.

"Hard pass on that guy, huh?"

The masculine voice comes from my left, and I jolt in surprise when I realize the question's directed at me. I've only been dimly aware of my fellow bar patrons, and I vaguely remember someone taking the stool beside me and ordering a Hendrick's martini with olives. But after he went with regular olives instead of the bartender's suggestion of bleu cheese olives, I hadn't given him another thought. I'm of the mindset that when an offer of cheese is on the table, the answer is always yes, so he failed my test he didn't even know he was taking.

But I'm regretting now that I didn't pay him more attention, because perhaps I'd have identified the fact that he is a *creep*. He's clearly been watching what I'm doing on my phone, and as far as I'm concerned, that should be illegal.

I very obviously, and yes, a bit passively aggressively, set my phone face down on the bar and pivot towards him.

"Seriously?" I say in my frostiest voice. I lift my wine glass and deliberately set my seething *oh no you didn't* glare at his elbow beside mine on the bar and let it travel slowly upwards, imagining burning through his suit sleeve with my indignant anger.

Finally, my eyes reach his.

Oh my.

My intentions of telling him off fly out the window when our gazes meet, because those are *nice*. Startlingly so. They're a delicious piercing blue, so cool they're nearly gray . . .

My stomach flips, and not in the good way.

I know those eyes. I *just* saw them. On TapThat.

The color drains from my face. Or maybe the color *floods* to my face, I'm not sure. All I know is I want to die, because the guy sitting beside me doesn't just *look* like the guy I'd just passed over on the dating app.

He *is* that guy.

And he's literally just watched me reject him outright.

To his credit, he doesn't put up a defensive smirk. Nor does he look annoyed, or pissed, or *hurt*, which would be worst of all.

Mostly he looks bemused by the entire situation, his eyebrows lifted in a silent challenge. *Well?*

I clear my throat as my brain scrambles for proper protocol in this situation. Bad move. The throat-clearing creates a throat tickle. One of those small but aggressive ones that come out of nowhere and make your eyes water as you cough in a futile attempt to soothe the tickle.

It's one of the few things in life that wine won't fix, and I look around for the bartender to beg for the water I'd declined when she'd offered it earlier.

The man rolls his eyes slightly at my frenzied hacking, and uses a single finger to push me his water glass. I gulp it frantically until the throat tickle abates, and set the empty glass back on the bar.

I give him what I hope is a grateful and charming smile. In the best of circumstances, I know my smile is rather charming. Or, at the very least, I like to think it's one of my best features.

Granted, the word used most often to describe my smile is *great*, or less flatteringly, *big*. Not pretty, or beautiful.

But it's toothy and bright, and when I shine it at people, even the grumpy ones tend to smile back.

Not so with this guy. Hmm.

My smile dims slightly, but I'm still determined to make amends. "So. Hi."

"Hello." His voice isn't quite unkind, just . . . bored.

Ouch. I am a lot of things, but I know I'm not boring. I turn towards him a little more fully, just in case he missed the fact that I'm wearing a lace bustier beneath my tuxedo-style blazer. For added good measure, I tuck my hair behind my ear, knowing it calls attention to my trademark blue streak at my temple that's a stark contrast to the platinum blonde of the rest of my head.

But the man's attention is back on his cocktail, and he misses the whole show. Fine. If he's not going to check me out, *I'll* study *him*.

I'll give the guy credit, he's better in person. His photo on TapThat didn't do justice to the Captain America vibes of his cheekbones and jawline, and it missed the ever-so-slight dent in his chin entirely.

Decent body, too. Not as big and broad as I like my guys, but neither is he short and scrawny. The way his suit jacket stretches across his shoulders is nice. Quite nice.

And yet . . . not my type. Not even a little bit. His haircut is short and boring, his gaze too direct, and he's wearing a suit. I hate guys in suits.

And then there's his *energy*. I'm big into noticing people's energy, and this guy gives off very quiet, intense vibes. Not at all laid-back-and-charming like I like 'em.

Yup. I made the right call in passing him over.

I just wish he hadn't *seen* me pass him over. I have plenty of flaws, but generally *rude* isn't on the list.

"So, you live in this neighborhood?" I ask brightly, going into full damage-control mode.

His storm-cloud eyes cut to mine, and for a second I feel something hot and intriguing pass through me, but I ignore it.

For an awful minute, I think he's going to ignore me, but then he sighs and answers. "No. East Side. You?"

"A couple blocks that way." I tilt my head in the direction of downtown. "What brings you over to the West Side?" This bar is decent. I've been here a handful of times. But only because it's so convenient to both my apartment and office. It doesn't have much to recommend it to someone not already in the neighborhood, especially in a town with about a billion bars and restaurants.

Before he can reply, the bartender comes over and gives me a bright smile. "Oh, hey! See, I *knew* he'd show."

"What?" I ask, confused, until I realize she thinks that this guy is my blind date. "Oh, no. No no. No, no no. *He* isn't my date."

Then I let out a little laugh because the man sitting beside me is just about as far from Kris Powers as it's possible to get.

The bartender makes a *whoops* face as she refills the guy's water glass that I'd emptied, and then hightails it to the other end of the bar.

The man beside me leans in ever so slightly. "I don't think you've made your lack of interest in me *quite* clear enough yet. Perhaps we could set up a sign of some sort? A *not if he was the last man alive* sort of message?"

I cringe and give him what I hope is a placating smile. "Listen, it's not personal, it's just . . ." I trail off, because there really is no way to tell someone they're not your type.

"Don't worry about it," he cuts in.

"It's nothing against you, it's just—"

"Let me guess," he says, turning fully towards me. "You prefer your dudes brawny and sulky? With bonus points if they're flexing in their photo, or better yet, displaying that stupid crotch V."

I choke on my wine. "Crotch V?"

"Different than a female crotch V," he says, with a flash of wicked smile that disappears so quickly I think I've imagined it. "V-cut, I believe it's called. You know what I'm talking about. Men who like to show off the shape wearing their gym shorts lower than necessary."

I fiddle with one of the three studs in my ear and bite the inside of my lip, because I *do* know exactly what he's talking about—the enticing V-cut groove running from the outer edge of a man's abs down towards his . . .

Well, let's just say I usually refer to the V-cut as dick lines.

I don't tell Mr. Stormcloud this.

Nor do I mention that Kris Powers had a very nice V-cut, or how disappointed I am not to be seeing the apex of that V tonight.

"Uh huh," he says knowingly, as though reading my thoughts.

"You know, if I can offer some friendly advice . . ." I start to say.

"I'd rather you did not."

I continue, undeterred. "You seem *awfully* irritable. Perhaps, rather than obsessing about other men's crotch Vs, you should care more about seeing a female crotch V. I find that such co-ed activities are instant mood boosters."

He snorts and nabs a non-bleu-cheese olive off the silver cocktail pick with straight, even teeth. "No, thanks."

My jaw drops open. "I wasn't *offering*. I didn't mean *my* crotch V."

He laughs and shakes his head. "Again. Just get a sign that you're not interested."

I sigh and set my wine aside. "Okay, let's start over. I'm Mac."

I extend my hand, and after a moment of hesitation, his closes around mine. Bigger and warmer than expected. "Thomas."

"No nickname?" I prod. "Tom?"

He shakes his head.

"Tommy?"

He gives me a look.

"Come on," I cajole with a smile. "What did your mom call you when you were little?"

"Thomas."

Good Christ. "Well, *Thomas*. What's your story? No, wait, I want to guess. New England born and bred. Yes?" I prod, when he doesn't reply.

He gives me an irritated look. "Boston."

"Ah ha. Which makes you a graduate of . . . Harvard?"

The guy practically smells like Ivy League.

"Dartmouth."

"Same thing. And before that, you went to a prep school that required a uniform and a tie." I don't bother waiting for him to confirm this, I'm fairly confident. "Let's see, what else? The oldest child."

His eyes narrow, and I give him a gloating smile.

"And—you iron your underwear. Which are tighty-whities." I say this to provoke him, but I confess, I'm the tiniest bit curious.

Unfortunately, he doesn't take the bait, and I'm oddly disappointed when Thomas reaches for the billfold that's been sitting in front of him, and he's apparently already closed out, because he pulls out a thick, black credit card and tucks it back into his wallet.

I watch as he adds a generous tip—hey, if he can creep on my phone, I can creep on his bill—and adds a messy, masculine scrawl to the bottom of the bill.

He stands and glances down at me, bored expression firmly in place.

"*Really* nice to meet you, Mac," he says dryly, as he slips his wallet back into an interior suit pocket.

I lift my wine glass in mocking acknowledgement, and I pick up my phone from the bar to see if TapThat #3 or #4 have tapped me.

I jump a little when I feel a warm hand press low on my back to get my attention. I turn my head towards Thomas, then freeze when I find his face is just inches from my own, his lips a whisper away.

Something unfamiliar and dangerous tingles down my spine at his closeness.

"Here's a quick fact about me that you missed, Mac," he says, and the crisp pronunciation of the ending *ck* sound of my name is borderline erotic.

He waits patiently for me to meet his gaze before delivering his parting barb with a cool smile: "I didn't tap you either."

CHAPTER TWO

Monday, September 12

~

I've never been that girl who rocks the whole early morning thing. For that matter, how old is too old to consider oneself a girl? Is twenty-eight too old?

Probably.

But considering I'm wearing bikini bottoms under my slacks because I forgot to do laundry, it's safe to say I'm not exactly crushing adulthood by most people's standards.

Let's just say, it's been *A Morning,* capital M. The kind where you snooze your alarm three times past *whoops*. Which means the shower is an "essentials only," no time for languishing. Blow dry? Nope. And though I always love taking time with my makeup, today, it's limited to a swipe of concealer beneath my eyes, and a dark red lipstick applied while navigating Manhattan foot traffic.

And even with all that rushing?

Late. I'm going to be late. Which, I'll be honest, isn't a completely uncommon occurrence, and usually it isn't even that big of a deal. I work at the global headquarters for a super-high-end jewelry brand, which you'd think would mean everything is very nine to five and by the book.

And maybe it is, in some departments. But I'm a graphic designer, and my team leans heavily into the eccentric creative stereotype. I've had one coworker who's been campaigning for years to be able to bring her cats to work because they center her aura. Another who has special goggles in the office to block out the "bad vibes" of the overhead fluorescents.

My tardiness is just not that big of a deal.

Usually. Today is different.

Today, my team of misfits gets a new boss—the next in a long line of senior managers who we've run off, not intentionally, just . . . well, see above about cats and goggles.

I work at Fifty-Ninth and Broadway, and the elevator ride up to the thirty-eighth floor makes a half-dozen stops and takes *forever*. I cross my toes inside my patent leather flats that the nine am staff meeting is off to a late start, but making my way towards my cubicle, I know I'll have no such luck. The floor is way too quiet.

Which means, my entire team is in the conference room to meet the new boss, and now I get to do a very special kind of walk of shame. I don't even have the trusty standby excuse of New Yorkers everywhere ("Grr! The damn subway!"), because everyone knows I walk the few blocks.

I mentally run through possible excuses, but I used up all the good ones in my repertoire when I was hooking up with a security guard in a nearby office building who worked the night shift. Our best chance at Sexy Times was in the tiny sliver of time between him leaving his shift and me getting into the office.

Even if that guy was still in the picture, I'm not sure I want to start off my first day with a new boss by alluding to morning sex excuses. I'm free-spirited, not nuts.

It doesn't help that Elodie's HQ is nearly as glitzy as the brand's stores and products. Everything from the cubicle dividers to the conference room walls are clear. Navigating around the office unnoticed isn't really an option.

Suck it up, Mac.

Dropping my stuff off at my cubicle, I speed-walk to the conference room, slowing down as I approach. All things considered, my entrance isn't as bad as it could be. The door doesn't squeak when I open it. *And* because there's so many people in the meeting today, they've brought in extra chairs, and I'm able to grab one right near the doorway. My new boss's boss is speaking, and seems wonderfully unaware of my late arrival.

Stevie—one of my fellow designers who's apparently decided to forgo his goggles for this morning's occasion—leans over. "Love the hair. Very mermaid."

I gently kick his calf. So much for hoping the dampness of my hair wasn't noticeable.

I pull the damp strands up into a messy bun and try to tune into Christina's recitation of the new boss's backstory, mostly listening for his name, which I've promptly forgotten from the email that came through last week. Blah blah, Summa Cum Laude Dartmouth, blah blah, the *linchpin* behind Cartier's supersuccessful TV spot . . . *Yawn.*

I'm more of a visual learner, so I shift in my chair, trying to get a peek at the new guy. Christina Riley, Elodie's creative director, must have invited everyone on the marketing team, not just the design crew, because the conference room's as packed as I've ever seen it, with the chairs surrounding the table three deep.

Figuring the man of the hour will be near Christina, I focus at the head of the table, looking for anyone I haven't seen around the office before.

I know her, seen him, hate *her . . .*

Then my gaze collides with stormy gray eyes, and my scanning gaze screeches to a halt along with my heart.

Mother of all living hell!

It's him. *Again.*

The very same man I'd rejected on the app.

The very same man who was sitting next to me as I did so.

Preston? Winston? Connery?

Thomas.

And just like that, the name of my new boss comes crashing back to me.

This is . . . not good.

Christina may be blissfully unaware of my late entrance, but I can tell from Thomas's unimpressed expression that he hasn't missed a thing. Not my damp hair, the late arrival. Hell, I feel like he even knows about the bikini bottoms I'm wearing because I forgot to do laundry. Which then makes me realize that the last conversation I had with this guy involved me referencing his tighty-whities.

No. This is not good *at all.*

"So," Christina is saying in a voice that's way too cheerful considering how my morning is going. "That's enough from me! Suffice to say, I speak on behalf of the entire team when I say we're so thrilled to have you join us, Thomas."

Yes. So thrilled, Thomas.

His gaze is still locked on me, and his eyes narrow ever so slightly, as though reading my sarcastic thoughts, before he shifts his attention back to Christina.

He stands and clears his throat. "I appreciate the warm welcome," Thomas says in that formal, clipped voice that's both sexier and more annoying than I remember. "I look forward to getting to know all of you. Specifically, I'm anxious to meet the talent that will be on my team, and Christina has generously given me use of the conference room for the rest of the morning for some one-on-one meetings."

Thomas picks up an iPad from the conference room table and glances down at it. "Let's do this the old-fashioned way, alphabetical by last name?"

I withhold my groan of dismay, but just barely.

Gray eyes flick to mine.

"Mackenzie Austin. Shall we start with you?"

CHAPTER THREE

Monday, September 12

*M*y coworkers file out of the conference room, many of them taking the extra chairs with them, and conversation has already shifted away from the new guy. I hear snippets of weekend recaps, grumbles about Monday, and frustrated gripes that senior leadership changed its mind *again* about the spring marketing campaign.

Take me with you!

Nobody seems aware of my inner agony, and far too quickly, I'm left all alone.

No, not alone. *He's* here.

Thomas has a blatantly bored expression on his face as he reads something on his phone, and for a horrific moment, I wonder if he even remembers me. Then he looks up, and suddenly the enormous conference room isn't nearly big enough for the two of us *and* our mutual antagonism.

He definitely remembers me.

Thomas nods to the chair immediately to his right and gives a slow, vaguely predatory smile. "Mac. Don't be a stranger. Not after all we've been through."

I grit my teeth and stand, not so much because my new *boss* has instructed it, but because I don't want to give him the satisfaction of thinking I'm avoiding him. I walk towards the head of the table, and he uses his foot to push a chair out for me.

I sit, and for a long moment we merely look at each other.

He's wearing a pinstripe navy suit, and I'm wondering if he got a haircut over the weekend in honor of his first day on a new job, because he looks even more obnoxiously Ivy League than he had on Friday night.

Also, his shoes have freaking tassels on them. I could *never* date a man with tassels. I nearly tell him this, then remember that we're not here as potential romantic partners. Not this time.

Thomas leans back in his chair, and though I suppose it could be construed as a relaxed gesture, there's something predatory about it. He pivots the chair slightly, resting an elbow on the conference room table as he studies me.

"So," I say, twisting one of my earring studs. "I guess now I know why you were in the neighborhood on Friday. Checking out the hood of your new office?"

Smoke & Baron, the bar where he and I met, is just one avenue over from the Elodie offices.

He lifts a shoulder, neither a confirmation or denial, then picks up his iPad from the table, glancing down. "Mackenzie Austin. AKA Mac." His gaze lifts again. "You put your nickname on your professional résumé?"

"Obviously."

His eyes narrow, and I try to remind myself that this is no

longer just some jerk at the bar, but the man who will determine my paycheck, my promotions, my very livelihood.

I smile. "You can call me Mackenzie if it makes you feel more comfortable, Thomas. Or should I call you Mr . . ."

"Decker," he says distractedly. "Thomas Decker."

Damn. It's a good name. I was hoping for something like Woodcock, or Spunkmeyer, or Seaman. You know, something I could really sink my mocking teeth into.

"You're a designer?" he asks, still scanning my résumé.

I nod. "I taught myself Photoshop in high school and sort of fell in love with it."

"No college?"

He asks it casually, not accusatorially, but my spine stiffens a bit anyway. "Wasn't really in the cards for me. But I've taken plenty of design classes in the city. And my work speaks for itself."

"I'm sure it does," he says noncommittally. "Christina speaks highly of you. You've been here longer than almost anyone else on the team."

I nod. "Diana, the senior copyeditor, started a few weeks before me, but we've both been here about six years."

"You like it?"

I give him a slight smile. "If I didn't, I certainly wouldn't tell my new boss on his first day."

"Why not? You don't seem the type to censor your thoughts."

"Well spotted," I say with a laugh. "And you're right. If I didn't like it, I'd probably blurt it out."

But I do like my job. Quite a bit, actually.

When I'd said I fell in love with Photoshop in high school, that was true, but that had really just been the start of it; my *crush* phase of loving all things design. I still use Photoshop, obviously, and a handful of other programs as well, but my work stopped being about my skill with certain apps a long time ago. For me, being a designer is just an ostentatious way of saying that I get paid for my imagination.

Yes, there's a lot of precision involved, which admittedly isn't usually my jam, but it's worth it to get to create something from nothing, to see something that lives in your head come alive on the computer screen. There's nothing quite like it. Especially now that I'm the *senior* designer on the team. I get to spend a lot more time with the concepts, and leave the pixel perfect stuff to Stevie and Monroe.

But here's a weird truth about me:

Sometimes I want to leave Elodie.

Not because I don't like my job, not because I'm not good at it.

But *because* I love it, *because* I'm good at it.

I've got the itchy sense that I'm betraying myself by staying in this cushy comfort zone. I feel at odds with myself, you know? I'm the woman who stays up too late, eats peanut butter Oreos for dinner way too often, who doesn't need or even want a guy to call the next day.

And yet when it comes to my professional life, I'm basically a white-picket-fence golden retriever suburbanite, in the form of a steady paycheck, a nine-to-five schedule, and a freaking health savings account.

I try not to think about it much, honestly. It's too uncomfortable, but for some reason this guy, the way Thomas looks at me, as though he sees all, and *judges* all, brings all those pesky, contradictory thoughts rushing forward. One more reason to dislike him.

"Okay, I have to ask," I say, shifting slightly in my chair, because bikini bottoms don't make for the most comfortable underwear substitute and we've got a real *riding up* situation, if you know what I'm saying.

"Is this going to be weird?" I continue.

"Is what going to be weird?" he asks. "The fact that you and I crossed paths in a dating app prior to working together?"

"*And* crossed paths in person," I point out.

Thomas shrugs indifferently. "I shouldn't think it'd be a problem. We didn't actually date. Neither has even a remote interest in the other, romantically speaking."

The calm way he says this chafes at my nerves. I hear no intent to insult, just a dispassionate stating of facts, which is somehow more insulting than if he'd taken a petty swipe.

"Will it be a problem for *you*?" he asks, looking so genuinely concerned at the prospect that I want to lean forward and strangle him.

"Of course not," I say with as much serenity as I can muster. "As far as I'm concerned, Friday night never happened."

"Excellent." He nods, as though the matter is settled. "I look forward to working together, Mac."

"And I look forward to working with you, Thomas," I say, matching his formality with just the tiniest bit of mockery that I'm pretty sure he notices and chooses to ignore.

He glances down at his list of new team members to meet. "Since I don't know where anyone sits yet, would you mind sending in Margaret Bleeker?"

"Love to," I say, meaning it. Margaret is the newest hire on the team, a very junior copyeditor fresh out of college, who is sweet and bubbly and never stops talking. She's going to drive Thomas *nuts*, and I almost wish I could stay to watch it.

I hesitate in the doorway, then turn back. "So, I promise, the moment I walk out this door, we'll never mention *it* again. But before we strike Friday from the record, can I ask one tiny question?"

"Sure," he replies after an infinitesimal pause.

There. That beat of hesitation, the flash of wariness is all I need to know that I'm not the only one thrown off by this strange twist of fate.

I ask my question in a rush. "Why didn't you tap on me? On the app? I don't care, I'm just curious."

Thomas sighs. "Mac—"

"Let me guess. You prefer brunettes."

"It's not—"

"Or," I interrupt. "You've got a thing for tall women."

I'm only 5'2.

"It's nothing that specific," he says, sounding annoyed. "It's just . . ." He breaks off, then shrugs. "It was just a *no chemistry* thing."

"Oh. Right, gotcha," I say, feeling stung, even as I try to remember that I'd had the same thought when I saw his picture.

I mime zipping my lips. "Okay, I have all the closure I need. Our lack of chemistry is to be mentioned never again."

"Good to know," he says with the slightest of eye rolls.

I exit the conference room, feeling mostly relieved, because uncomfortable as that whole thing was, it could have gone so much worse given the circumstances.

But then I turn my head slightly towards the conference room door, and our eyes lock through the glass.

Relief goes out the window, because for a strange moment, my stomach seems to turn over on itself.

I jerk my gaze away, telling myself it's irritation, not butterflies.

And yet, as I walk back to my desk, I can't shake the suspicion that Thomas might be terribly, horribly *wrong* about our lack of chemistry.

CHAPTER FOUR

Monday, September 12

～

"*Duuuuuuude*," my coworker says a couple hours later, draping herself dramatically over my desk. Her curly black hair blocks the screen of my Mac—yes, I *too* love that my nickname matches my Apple computer—as she fans herself. "Is it just me or is the new boss really hot?"

I use my pen to push her hip off my trackpad so her butt quits wreaking havoc on my attempts to digitally place an engagement ring on top of a tulip in a way that doesn't look completely ridiculous.

Sadie Washington started at Elodie a year after me, as a UX designer. Her job is to ensure that things make sense as well as look pretty. She's also my closest friend on the team—my work wife, so to speak.

Sadie is loyal, irreverent, and funny as heck, with a thing for emo guys from Brooklyn. She actually has a points system for men; for example, guys get bonus points if they pair skinny jeans *and* thick black-rim glasses and have some sort of botanical tattoo.

Like me, she's got a type, and like me, that type is not Thomas Decker, so I'm genuinely surprised by her proclamation of his hotness.

I'm genuinely surprised by her interest in our new boss.

"Really?" I ask her, wrinkling my nose. "Did you put your contacts in today?"

"Oh, come on. You don't see it?" she demands. "I just had my one-on-one with him, and I have no idea what he said, because oh my god, those eyes!"

"They're very . . . intense," I agree.

"Um, yeah. *Intense* in the way where you can just imagine him lifting you up and taking you on the—"

"Nope. Nope, nope, nope and *eeew*, Sade. Since when have uptight preppy guys done it for you? The last guy you dated had a French braid and wore velvet pants unironically."

"Arkin," she says with a dreamy sigh. "He filled out those pants nicely."

"See, there you go. Trust me, you're much better lusting after Velvet Pants than our new boss."

Sadie flicks her fingers as though shaking off powdered sugar from a doughnut. "Arkin's old news. He developed a crush on his new neighbor, some little waif of a thing who probably has a lot more patience for listening to his terrible poems than I did."

"I thought you liked poetry."

"Me too." She picks up my stapler and studies it. "Apparently I only like the *idea* of poetry."

Sadie sets the stapler aside and crosses her feet at the ankle, settling all the way on my desk. "Okay, your turn. How'd it go on Friday night? With the Kyle guy from the gym."

"Kris," I say. "And he stood me up."

She gives an outraged gasp. "He did not."

"He did," I say with a shrug, since the sting of that rejection has been distinctly muted by the fresh wave of horror brought on by the Thomas Decker interaction that had followed.

"Well, that sucks," she says, patting my head, a bit like I'm a dog, and I sort of see why dogs like it. Very soothing. "But look at the bright side, we're both single at the same time, and per our pact . . . Tequila Tuesday tomorrow?"

"Done," I say immediately. It'll give me a safe place and some liquid courage to fill her in on the disastrous TapThat encounter with the new boss.

I haven't told anyone, not Collette or my mom, and I tell them pretty much everything. But Collette is a romantic, and will probably try to tell me that it was a case of kismet or something. And my mom, guaranteed, will barely let me finish the story before relaying some story of her own that echoes mine, but even more crazy. That's kind of my mom's thing—no matter what experience I lay at her feet, no matter how crazy, she always has a story that's even crazier, and oh yeah, happened first.

But I need to talk to someone about this whole Thomas mess, and it can't be here or now. Elodie has an open floor plan, only the senior managers and above have offices with doors.

Plus, Piers, the technical designer I share a cubicle wall with, loves gossip. Last week, he tried to drag the water cooler from the kitchen to his cubicle after being convinced he was missing out on the "hot goss."

"Ooh!" Sadie jumps and then leans forward, reaching beneath her butt and pulling out my vibrating cell phone. "That was a zippy buzz in a special place. Here you go! Mama Annette is calling."

I take the phone, about to lift it to my ear when I remember it's just buzzed Sadie's "special place," and instead pop in my Air-Pods to take the call.

Sadie hops off my desk and waggles her fingers as she saunters off.

"Hey, Mom, what's up?" I'm genuinely curious. My mom and I talk often, almost daily, but her calling before noon is practically unheard of.

"Hey, baby! Where are you, whatcha doin'?"

"At work," I say, grabbing my tin of fancy Earl Grey out of my desk drawer and heading to the kitchen to make my usual late morning cup of tea.

I'm careful to keep the edge out of my response, but I feel a little flicker of irritation all the same. I've had the same corporate job for six years. That's more than *a thousand* nine-to-five work days, and yet Mom always seems to think that on any given Monday I might be on a yacht, or in the jungle, or cozied up in bed with a Hollywood stuntman.

Case in point . . .

I hear a murmur of hushed voices and what sounds like a rustle of sheets, followed by the petulant, masculine groan of a man who was hoping to get laid and didn't.

Yuck. I mean, yay Mom for having a healthy sex life, but mostly *yuck*.

"Sorry, what did you ask?" she asks into the phone.

"You asked how I was," I point out patiently, as I step into the empty kitchen. "I said I'm at work."

She makes a tsking noise. "Always with that. You work too hard!"

I set the tea tin on the counter with a bit more force than necessary and again, try to shove away my irritation. Mom doesn't mean to annoy me. In fact, I'm sure she thinks she's being supportive.

But comments like that scrape at my emotions all the same.

It's not as though I'm some sort of uptight workaholic daughter trying to rebel against my bohemian mother. I work the *normal* amount. Enough to pay my bills—for that matter, enough to pay *her* bills some months.

I can afford to buy decent toilet paper, and go out for the occasional Tequila Tuesday, and yeah, I splurge on this fancy tea because the generic stuff they keep stocked in the kitchen tastes like dirt-water.

But it's not like I'm a perfectionist. I show up late. I sometimes leave early. I have virtually no respect for authority.

And yet in my mother's mind, working "too hard" means working *at all.* To her, life that's not one big constant party is, her words, a "major bummer."

"It's 10:30am on a Monday. A pretty normal time to be at work." I say this as gently as possible. I don't want to crush my mom's free spirit, just sort of . . . corral it for the sake of my own sanity.

"Which is why you need a job where you make your own hours!" she says in a bright voice. I hear the beep of her coffee machine in the background. "Which reminds me, have I told you about this virtual assistant course?"

There it is.

You'd think that knowing it's coming would mean it doesn't faze me, but somehow, despite the fact that I've been dealing with this routine of ours for a decade doesn't take the sting out it. Even though I'm twenty-eight and should know better, there's still a *little* part of me that wants her to call because she wants to know what's up with me. Not just because she needs something.

And more often than not, what she needs ends up having a detrimental effect on my bank account. An "investment opportunity" here, a reminder that *in order to make money, you have to spend money!* there . . .

"Hmm, no, I don't think you've mentioned it," I say, dropping a tea bag into one of the company mugs.

"Okay, well, Janine—you remember her, from that physical therapy training class I started, but then had to quit because the teacher was a jerk? Anyway, Janine's taken this class about being a virtual assistant—a VA, they're called. And now she said she's looking at making six figures this year. Can you even believe it?"

It's a rhetorical question, so I ignore it and get straight to the point. "How much does the training cost?"

"I'll message you a link with all the details, and baby, of course you know it would be a loan! Once I finish the course, I'll make back the cost immediately and will reimburse you every penny and then some."

Uh huh. I've heard that one before. A lot.

"Sure, send me the details," I say. "But I've gotta get back to work."

Then, realizing that'll just be fuel for her work-too-hard protests, I tack on a lame excuse. "I've got a new boss—a by-the-book type."

"Oh, you didn't tell me you had a new boss. What was the old one's name? Peter?"

"Louise," I reply. I don't think I even *know* a Peter, but I guess at least she's pretending to act interested.

"The new one's a dick, huh?" she asks, as I hear the clank of a coffee mug on her end.

"Eh. He's alright." I add hot water to my mug. "Just super uptight and corporate."

"Ugh, that's the *worst*," she says with genuine feeling, and I have to smile, because my mom's the least corporate person you can imagine. I can at least fake it, but I'm pretty sure she'd straight up wither at the mere sight of a cubicle wall. It's one of the things I love about her, even when she drives me crazy.

"Okay, well, I'll let you go, sweetie. Look out for that link about the training!"

"Will do," I promise, just a touch tiredly. "Love you."

I hang up the phone and turn to head back to my desk only to go still when I realize I'm not alone in the kitchen.

"You," I say. "Again."

"Me," Thomas says, matching my inflectionless tone. "Again."

He walks calmly to the fancy coffee machine and sets a mug in place, punching a button.

Other than when he was behind me at the bar—*when he touched my back*—this is the first time I've seen him standing up. He's not the tallest man I've ever seen, but there's a fit athleticism about him that doesn't quite meld with the shrimpy, bookish identity I've created for the guy.

To make myself feel better, I look down at his feet, hoping to reassure myself with those stupid tassels, but they do nothing to make me feel better.

I hate this day.

I swallow and tap the edge of my phone against my mug lightly. Nervously. "It was my mom. I always feel guilty not picking up."

"Ah yes. Must appease mothers," he murmurs noncommittally.

"You have one?" I blurt out.

His eyebrows go up. "Do I have a mother? Exactly how *corporate* am I that you think I wasn't born to a human female?"

I purse my lips. "So. You heard my conversation."

"Small room," he says, gesturing around, then taps his ear. "Perfect hearing."

Shit.

"Look, it wasn't—"

"It's fine," he cuts in, his face never changing expression. "Forget it."

Thomas starts to exit the kitchen, and I step towards him quickly. "You're not going to fire me, are you? Because I said you were boring and corporate?"

His eyes cut to mine. "Well, your actual words were *uptight* and corporate. But I'll be sure to add *boring* to the list of my attributes, according to Mackenzie Austin."

I exhale and close my eyes. "Any chance you have a shovel? Something I can use to dig my way out of this?"

His lips twitch slightly. "Sorry. No."

"*Awesome*," I say with feeling. I point to the door. "Sooooo, I'm gonna head back to my desk now?"

"An excellent idea."

I speed-walk out of the kitchen, but before I can round the corner to safety . . .

"Mac," he says again.

I turn.

"My mother," he says. "Her name is Mary. I feel guilty not picking up her phone calls too."

Well, well. Looks like he's at least part human after all.

I give him a wide smile. "Would she like me? I bet she would like me."

Thomas rolls his eyes. "Goodbye, Mac."

But he's smiling a little as he says it. I count it as a win.

CHAPTER FIVE

Friday, September 16

⟳

*M*y best friend in the entire world is Collette Burton, who's about as different from me as it's possible to get.

For starters, she's tall, elegant, and has *really* shiny brown hair. The first two are God-given, the third has a little help from her fancy SoHo salon. She's an associate at some fancy downtown law firm, rocks four-inch stilettos no matter the time of day, and would never, *ever* have to wear bikini bottoms because she forgot to do laundry.

In fact, she probably wouldn't own a bikini—she's more of a classic one-piece kind of girl, even though she works out six days a week and has Victoria's Secret model-worthy boobs.

In other words, she's very, very easy to hate, but luckily, even easier to love. We met at a mutual friend's party in our early twenties, bonded over our shared love of the Indiana Jones franchise, and somehow we just kept hanging out until we became the biggest part of each other's life.

Well, we *used* to be the biggest part of each other's life.

Now, my darling Collette has found herself a man.

I'm not bitter about it, not really. In fact, I'm pretty proud. I always knew that Collette would get married some day, but I figured she'd do it in a Collette kind of way: Meet *the* guy. Know he was perfect right away, but not sleep with him until the fifth date. Then, make him go on a billion more dates over the course of two years. Move in with him, to make sure they were compatible. Another two years. Eventually, an engagement that would last *another* two years, in order to pull off the City's Most Perfect Wedding.

Instead, Collette went and pulled a Mac. My risk-averse, owns-multiple-planners best friend has finally done something spontaneous:

She's marrying a guy she's only been seeing for three months.

Jonathan is a fellow lawyer at her firm, and even I as a romance-skeptic can see that he's perfect for her. In addition to being every bit as beautiful as she is, he's smart and sweet. But not the sugar kind of sweet, the right amount. Plus, Jon makes Collette laugh, and I *do* love a man who can make my best friend laugh.

Even better, he's also extremely tolerant of her flighty, often-late best friend.

Because yes, I am just the *teensiest* bit late to their engagement party.

Though for once, it's truly not my fault: Sixth Avenue was closed due to some sort of manhole incident, which means the cab driver had to go the *lonnnnng* way around to get to the fancy Astor Room just off Park Avenue.

Collette comes from an upper-middle-class family in Connecticut, and though I don't know much about Jonathan's family, at first glance at the party attendees, it's pretty obvious that they too come from money. I spot enough red soles on the women's shoes to rival the Louboutin section at Bergdorf's.

And all of the men's suits have that custom made look to them. Not because I know about fashion, but because designers have an eye for stuff that looks good, and these people all look really good. And expensive.

Everyone also seems to be extremely tall.

Even my high heels (*not* Louboutins, in case you were wondering), the search for my best friend in the crowded room is not going well on account of all the shoulders at my eye level. Finally, I spot her standing over by the dessert table, looking flawless and bridal in a strapless white cocktail dress and pale pink pumps with little bows on the heels. She spots me and grins. Collette whispers something to Jon, who nods and removes his hand from her waist.

I'm delighted to note the way his gaze follows his fiancée as she heads towards me, adoring and just a little bit hungry. That's exactly the way a man *should* look at his future wife, and I'm thrilled Collette's found it. And even though that's not in the cards for me—my choice—sometimes I wonder what it would be like. To have someone look at me that way . . .

"Hi!" Collette says, enveloping me in a one-armed, Chanel-scented hug, since the other is holding a flute of champagne. "You made it!"

"Of course I made it! What are maids of honor for?" I say, giving her a tight squeeze.

"Oh, so!" she says, pulling back, her eyes glowing with excitement and maybe a little of the bubbly in her glass. "That reminds me, on my way to work I passed the new shop for this up-and-coming designer, and I saw this navy dress that would be so perfect on you. Do you have time later this week to go take a look? I want to make sure you're wearing something you love."

"Of course! I know I'll love it." Even if I don't, for Collette, I'd wear a dirty garbage bag.

A tuxedo-clad server comes over with a tray of champagne, and Collette exchanges her almost-empty for a fresh one, and grabs another for me.

"Okay, so who are all these people?" I ask in a whisper. Collette's got a decent-sized extended family, but I'm estimating that there are well over a hundred people spanning a couple different rooms.

"So much for the low-key intimate party, right?" she says with a little laugh. "Basically, you're looking at every Burton who was ever born. And Mom's family flew down from Toronto, so there's that. Plus, I think *all* of our colleagues RSVP-ed yes, so we've got the entirety of Stanley and Summers in the room."

Collette scans the crowd, mentally cataloging the remaining guests. "The rest is Jon's side, though that's a pretty small group—he doesn't have a ton of extended family. Oh, and that reminds me," she says, craning her neck to look for someone. "I've got to introduce you to Jon's brother. The best man."

"Please tell me he's not as gorgeous as Jon. I don't want him overshadowing me in pictures," I joke.

"He's pretty cute, but so are you. I even thought about fixing you up, but he showed up with a date. Ah! There he is."

Collette's fingers wrap around my wrist, pulling me forward

through the crowd. Since she's seven inches taller than me, her shoulder blades block my view as we weave through the crowd.

So it's not until we reach her fiancé and she steps aside that *it* happens.

Déjà vu, and not the good kind.

I faintly listen to Collette make introductions, but unfortunately, they're entirely unnecessary.

Gray eyes blink once in surprise as they lock on mine, and then Thomas Decker lets out the smallest of irritated sighs. "You have *got* to be kidding me."

CHAPTER SIX

Friday, September 16

⌒

"*T*his is my nightmare," I mutter into my champagne.

"Sorry?" Collette says, sharing a bemused look with Jon. "What are we missing?"

Oh, where to start.

I exchange a glance with Thomas. *You want to take this one?*

There's the briefest moment of camaraderie that we're in this strange mess together, but he stays silent, so I take a sip of my champagne and break the news to the group. "Thomas here is actually my new boss."

"Wait, seriously?" Jon says with a laugh. "Oh man. I can't believe I didn't make that connection when you told me you took the job at Elodie."

Thomas takes an insultingly large swallow of his cocktail in response.

I notice that he doesn't mention that actually we'd met *before* he showed up as my new boss, and it doesn't seem like he brought his brother up to speed on the encounter.

I can't decide if I'm relieved or insulted.

Either way, I guess I can't judge him. I still haven't told Collette. She's been crazy busy with the prep for the party tonight, plus I still haven't felt up for her inevitable serendipity spin on the whole thing. Though, I have to admit, she might have a point there. What are the odds in a city this big that I'd encounter the same man three times in a single week?

And not just glancing encounters. Two out of the three (him being my boss, and my best friend's future husband's brother) are sort of lasting entanglements.

As for the first . . .

All of a sudden, I remember Collette said that Thomas had a date, and I shift my attention to the woman standing beside him.

"Hey, I'm Mac," I introduce myself cheerfully. Partly to be friendly, and . . . yeah, okay, no. I'm just suffering from *raging* curiosity.

"Hi there. Anna," she says with a friendly smile, shaking my hand.

Anna is pretty. Very pretty. Medium height, perfect posture, and she has good skin—ugh, nothing more annoying than girls with good skin. She also seems genuinely nice. Her smile crinkles her eyes in a really cute way, which tells me she's way too good for Thomas, whose glower is so pointed I can practically feel my profile getting frostbite.

I'm dying to ask Anna how long she's known Thomas and to blink twice if she's here against her will, but Collette interjects. "This is seriously such a small world," she says, looking between me and Thomas.

"This will actually work out great," Jon adds enthusiastically.

"Since you'll see each other at work, it'll be easier to coordinate the bachelor–bachelorette party."

Oh, hell.

Jon and Collette let me know last week that they'd decided to do a joint bachelor and bachelorette party, and though it meant I'd have to temper the rowdy, stripper-focused party I'd dreamed of for my best friend, I'd actually been sort of grateful to have a planning partner in the process, since *ahem*, planning is not exactly my thing.

But co-planning with *him*?

Haven't I been punished enough?

Plus, if Thomas has it his way, we'll probably all end up at a lacrosse or polo tournament with Scotch for the men and white wine spritzers for the ladies.

Something tells me Thomas Decker isn't going to be as excited as me about the assortment of male-genitalia candy I found online.

"I am ecstatic," Thomas says, and though I roll my eyes at the exceedingly thick layer of sarcasm, nobody else seems to notice.

"Thomas, Mac has such a good eye for design," Collette is gushing. "But then, you already know that, I guess, if you've seen any of her work. But I'm talking like, life stuff too. You should see her home, it looks like a perfect Pinterest board. And I'd kill for her fashion sense."

I love my best friend, but I'm wishing she wouldn't have said that, because now I feel everyone inspecting my chosen outfit for the evening. The reactions are varied.

Anna: Polite curioisty.

Collette: Sisterly pride.

Jon: Brotherly indifference.

Thomas . . .

Well, let's just say the way he looks at me makes me regret that I didn't stick with the conservative cocktail dress that had been my safe plan B. Instead, I went with my gut-reaction A plan: I've paired a full black tulle skirt with a lace-trimmed camisole that's a near-neon shade of pink.

In front of my full-length mirror at home, I'd felt sexy and fashion-forward. Under Thomas's withering gaze I feel like a little kid playing dress-up.

Especially standing beside the two suit-wearing men and Collette's timeless classiness. Even Anna, who's never met the bride and groom before now, seems to have better sense than me. Thomas's date's attire is the very definition of the little black dress; flattering without being showy, stylish without standing out from the crowd.

"You look great, Mac. As always," Jon says kindly.

"I'm *obsessed* with that skirt," Anna says with that genuine niceness again. "I wouldn't even know where to find something like that." She gives a self-deprecating laugh. "Not like I could pull it off."

"You look beautiful," Thomas tells her. A little stiffly, in my opinion, but she blushes a little and looks pleased.

I notice he doesn't tell me I look beautiful. In fact, he doesn't look my way at all.

Conversation shifts to wedding stuff, the way it often does in Collette's orbit these days. Anna is all about it, asking all the right questions about colors and cake flavors and the honeymoon. As maid of honor I know I should chime in, but . . .

I need a minute.

I need a minute to wrap my head around the fact that my *boss* is going to be part of my best friend's family.

I touch Collette's arm and in a silent best-friend exchange indicate that I'll be back in a minute. *Okay?* She smiles and nods. *No prob!*

I don't have a destination or plan other than getting away from Thomas, and I'm grateful when I spot Eileen and Gary Burton waving me over. I haven't spent all that much time with them, but Collette's invited me to their place in Connecticut for their annual Fourth of July party, and they've invited me to join them for dinner when they come into the city to see Collette.

They're really formal. I don't think I've ever seen Eileen without her red lipstick and diamond earrings, and Gary wears pastel sweaters with the arms draped over his shoulders non-ironically. But it's a friendly kind of formal. I get the sense that maybe my blue hair streak and multiple earrings confused them at first, but they've never made me feel *less than*.

Which is more than I can say about Thomas. He's formal as well, but definitely not the friendly kind.

I hug the exuberant Eileen and Gary. I'm pleased to see they don't seem even remotely bothered by the short engagement, but then, how can they be when Jon's probably their dream son-in-law? They're sweet, asking me how I am, showing genuine interest in how work's been going, but after the fifth or so interruption from other guests wanting to congratulate the parents of the bride, I slip away, unnoticed.

I haven't finished my champagne, but it's a little warm, and I'm not into it, so I ditch it on a table and go to the open bar where I order a vodka tonic.

Through the crowd I see a glowing Collette surrounded by her coworkers, and knowing she doesn't need me right now, I slip out onto the patio. It's probably *the* place to be during spring and summer, but on a chilly fall evening, it's too cold to be comfortable.

Bonus though, that means I have the space entirely to myself. There are a few tables, but obviously they're not intended for use, because the chairs are turned upwards, stacked atop the table.

I pull one down and sit.

I exhale slowly, sip my drink and relish the relative quiet.

I'm actually a pretty social creature—not usually the wall-flower type.

But I also love moments like this one. Those rare moments, where you find unexpected little pockets of peace in noisy Manhattan. Moments where you're not *quite* alone—I can see dozens of people through the windows, hear their laughter, hear the band—and yet you've found a place of stillness and solitude.

I close my eyes and just enjoy it—the sense of being a part of something and simultaneously apart. There's a magic to it.

"May I join you?"

My eyes fly open, and of course—*of course*—it's *him* that destroys the solitude.

"Sure," I say, torn between resentment that my solitude was interrupted, and curiosity as to why he didn't go running the other way the moment he spotted me.

"Are you following me?" I ask, eyes narrowed slightly.

"Yes, Mac," Thomas says, his voice dry as dust as he pulls down a chair for himself. "I thought to myself, 'I haven't run into that woman nearly enough over the course of the past week, I *must* seek her out.'"

"Ha, ha," I reply, my voice just as dry as his. "Seriously. Why are you out here?"

"Same reason as you, I suppose," he says, setting his glass on the table and spinning it idly. "Fresh air. To take a moment."

"What about your girlfriend?" I ask.

His gaze flicks up. "I don't know that I'd call her that."

I lift my eyebrows. "You bring a woman to your brother's engagement party, but she's not your girlfriend?"

"Our second date was Wednesday. We had a good time, so I asked her out on Friday, forgetting it was the night of Jon's engagement party. I didn't want to back out of the commitment, so I invited her."

"Whew." I fan myself. "Romantic."

His jaw tenses. "At least *my* dates don't stand me up."

I flinch. "Touché."

He sighs and rubs the back of his neck. "I'm sorry. That was uncalled for."

"Little bit." I crunch a piece of ice between my molars.

He looks at me curiously. "The guy ever call? Text? Apologize in any way?"

"No." I stare down at the lemon wedge bobbing in my drink. "But I barely knew him, so my heart's still in one piece." I tap the left side of my chest as I say it, and I swear his gaze lingers, just a bit.

"Is your heart often in pieces?"

"Oh, god no," I reply, genuinely horrified. "I don't really do that whole thing."

He frowns in confusion. "What *thing*? Date?"

"I date a ton," I say. "I just don't let my heart get involved. Or rather, it's not a matter of *letting* it so much as . . ." I shrug. *It just never happens.*

He blinks. "Ever?"

I shrug indifferently. "What about you?"

Thomas sips his drink. "What about me?"

"Does your heart get involved when you date?"

He lets out a low whistle. "We've gotten deep rather fast, haven't we?"

"Well, our relationship is on an accelerated schedule." I smile. He smiles back, just a little.

"So," I prod, genuinely curious now. "Your heart?"

Thomas takes his time thinking. He takes his time with everything, as far as I can tell. "I think that's the point of dating, isn't it? To find someone you can get involved with, but won't—how did you phrase it? Leave your heart in pieces?"

"Disagree," I say confidently, shaking my head. "Or at least, that's not the reason *I* date."

"What's your reason?"

I waggle my eyebrows suggestively, playfully, though the searing look he gives me in return is anything but playful, and I look quickly away, pretending fascination with the view of the city.

"So who was the guy?" Thomas asks after a minute. "The no-show?"

He sounds genuinely curious, so I shrug and answer truthfully. "A trainer at my gym."

"I knew it. He *did* have a V-cut."

I let out a regretful sigh. "I saw hints. But I'll never get the chance to find out the real deal."

"Overshare. But that's your type, huh? Brawny beefcake?"

"Yeah," I say. "You were actually pretty dead on with your guess that night. Bad boys make my knees weak. And if there are tattoos and a bit of facial hair scruff, I'm a *total* goner."

"Even if the man can't master the calendar or have the decency to let you know he can't make it? Surely you can do better."

Darn. And we were doing so well, and then he has to go and get all uppity.

I let my gaze cool. "Don't let me keep you from rejoining your date. *Boss.*"

My snippy words are timed perfectly with the wind picking up, and I shiver a little, my camisole not providing any protection whatsoever against the chill.

Thomas pushes back his chair to stand, and I think he's read my dismissal loud and clear. But he surprises the hell out of me by shrugging out of his suit jacket and holding it out for me to take.

"Oh!" I'm startled by the gesture. A little appalled, and a little something else too. *Touched?* "No, I'm okay, thanks." My voice is almost panicked.

Instead of replying, he comes around the table and pulls the coat around my shoulders. Immediately I'm enveloped in warmth and a very expensive-smelling male scent.

I narrow my eyes. "It's not going to make me like you more, you know."

"Noted." He sits down again instead of leaving, and I hate that I'm a little happy about that. "But if I ever decide to stop being boring and uptight, you'll be the first to know."

"Okay, you *have* to let that go," I say, holding up a finger. "You were eavesdropping when I said that, so you got the intel through shady means."

"But you still said it," he says softly.

I swallow, because I have this awful feeling, like maybe I hurt him somehow, when I'd called him boring.

Guilt makes me defensive, and I force a smile. "I'm sure you don't exactly go running around singing *my* praises. I mean, if you were to talk to Mary about me, what would you say? Probably that I'm a hot mess?"

He doesn't reply for a few moments, and when he speaks again, it's to change the subject.

"How did you and Collette meet?" he asks. "You two seem . . ."

"Like the odd couple? A little bit. We met at a mutual friend's birthday a few years ago, and for whatever reason, we just clicked." I tilt my head and study him. "What about you and Jon? How much older are you?"

He looks bemused. "My mother would tell you it's rude to enquire about someone's age."

"I think Mary would tell you that only applies to women. Also, do I look like the type of person to lose sleep over proper manners?"

"True, you did reject me right in front of my face," he says, though his smile is a little more relaxed now.

"Only because I didn't know you were there!" I say, feeling my cheeks heat at the uncomfortable memory. Actually, everything related to this man seems to involve an uncomfortable memory. Including, increasingly, this conversation.

I try to bring us back around to safer topics once more. "So. Jon is the younger brother, or . . ."

He rolls his eyes at my persistence. "I'm two years older."

"And you guys are . . . the same? Different? Are you competitive? Best friends?"

"We're . . . brothers. We get along. Love each other. And yeah, Jon and I are pretty similar, but our younger brother Aaron is a bit of the black sheep."

"Meaning he went to Harvard instead of Dartmouth?"

Thomas snorts. "More like high school dropout who moved to Silicon Valley, launched a ridiculously successful video game platform that makes him worth more than Jon and me combined."

"Oh. Jeez. You jealous?"

Thomas doesn't hesitate. "Not even a little bit."

He looks away, reconsidering. "Well. Actually. Perhaps I envy Aaron's spontaneity. But I don't begrudge him the success, or the money. He worked hard and earned it. Jon and I work hard too, though I'd say we're both more rule followers. Jon's maybe a little more relaxed about it than me."

"*Whaaaaaat?*" I say, in fake surprise. "I'm totally shocked to hear you're not the relaxed type," I say, taking a sip of my drink.

Thomas opens his mouth, but before he replies, the sound of the party grows louder as the door to the patio opens, and Jon sticks his head out. "Hey, guys. I'm glad you're bonding and all, but pictures are about to be taken, and your presence is requested by my bride-to-be."

Thomas looks at me, tilting his head towards the door. "Shall we?"

"We shall," I say, matching his perfect, proper diction as I stand.

He motions me to precede him, and as I pass, Thomas reaches

out a hand, as though to place his palm on my back the way he had that first night at the bar.

He jerks it back, frowning as though puzzled by his own instincts.

I'm puzzled too, not because he didn't touch me.

But because I wanted him to.

CHAPTER SEVEN

Monday, September 19

⁓

*U*gh. *Ugh.*

It's official. I'm not twenty-two anymore, and my days of leaning hard into "Sunday-Funday" without repercussions are officially behind me. I spent yesterday with my friend Danielle, who of all my friends is the biggest party girl. Unlimited mimosas at brunch had stupidly turned into an afternoon at a wine bar, and though I'd wisened up enough to switch to club soda by the time we met up with a few more friends in the Village for an early dinner, the damage had been done.

So now it's Monday morning, and *my.head.hurts.*

It's not the worst hangover I've ever had, and I'm wearing clean underwear instead of bikini bottoms. So, a *slight* improvement over this time last Monday.

But if I'm going to survive five days a week with Thomas Decker as my boss, I need to do better than slight improvement. I need to bring my A-game all the time. I'm not off to a good start, and I'm annoyed with myself for making some rather irresponsible choices.

I'm also annoyed with myself for being annoyed with myself. Honestly? I used to relish this lifestyle, it was part of being young, and fun, and Mac. Even when I wanted to die from a hangover, at least I knew I'd had a good time the night before.

Now, I'm just fantasizing about Gatorade and Advil and making better choices in the future. That's new. And irritating.

Speaking of irritating . . .

New York City has the gall to be sunny today, so my walk to work is bright and aggravating. I manage a sunny fake smile for Angeline, the building security guard, and let out a grateful sigh as I step into the dimness of the elevator.

I'm shoving my sunglasses onto my head just as the closing elevator doors pop open again and someone else steps into the small space.

At my best, I *might* have been able to bite back my groan, but I think we've established that today is not my best, and the groan that escapes is pure aggravation. *Seriously?*

Thomas's cool gaze flicks briefly to the sunglasses now tangled in my hair, then drops to my face. The way he searches my features is brief, but telling. I have the unnerving, annoying sense that he's doing a scan of my operating system and has sussed out that a warning light is blinking. Status: *needs maintenance*.

"Good morning, Mackenzie."

"Mac," I say, giving in to the urge to pull my sunglasses back down onto my face. I'm staring stubbornly at the closing doors, I *feel* his smirk before he speaks.

"So. How was your weekend?"

"Really fantastic, thank you."

Thomas turns towards me, adjusting the strap of his computer bag on his shoulder. "Do you drink coffee?"

"I have a pulse, so yup."

"A triple mocha with whipped cream always does it for me. And a bagel with cream cheese."

I spare him a glare. "Does what for you?"

"See, usually I'm an oatmeal and take my coffee with just a splash of milk kind of guy," he continues. "But every now and then . . ."

Ah. I follow now. Thomas is sharing his hangover cure. I'm both surprised that he even has one, and . . . Nope, that's it. No *and.* I'm surprised, period. He doesn't look like the type to make, well, *mistakes.* Of any kind.

I could, of course, deny my current state; blame my lack of pep on a migraine or stomach bug. And I do consider it briefly, both for my pride and because he's my boss.

But quite frankly, I can't muster the energy to lie, so I let out a weary sigh.

"I'll keep the bagel and mocha recommendation in mind," I say. "I just have to survive a meeting first."

"With Christina," he says, as the elevator doors open.

"Right," I say in surprise, dropping my glasses back into my purse. "You keep track of my calendar?"

"I was on the invite as well."

"Oh." *Wonderful.* "And I didn't think my morning could get any better."

Thomas wisely ignores my grumpy sarcasm as we step off the elevator and head towards his boss's boss's office.

"Do you have meetings with Christina often?" he asks.

"I wouldn't say often, but it's not uncommon, either. Whenever the senior manager position—your position—is vacant, I report directly to her."

"It's been vacant a fair amount over the past couple of years, hasn't it?" he asks, glancing down at me.

There's curiosity in his voice, and I can't blame him. Overall, the design team doesn't have much turnover. Other than a senior copyeditor who left just after I started to be a stay-at-home-dad, and a UX designer who was only here a month before deciding to go freelance, our team's pretty stable.

The one exception is the role of my boss—we've had three senior managers in two years. Which makes it sound like we must be a nightmare to supervise, but I don't think that's it. Jo-Ellen was great, but she left because her wife got a last-minute job opportunity in Dallas that they couldn't pass up. Eli was also great, but had a distinctly entrepreneurial bent, and jumped at the chance to launch some sort of gaming app in Silicon Valley. Most recently, Shelly had been less great, and now that I think about it, we *may* actually have run her off because she was the worst.

"Apparently, it's not exactly anyone's dream job," I admit.

"Not yours, anyway."

I stop walking. "What's that supposed to mean?"

He stops and turns toward me. "Christina mentioned on my first day that she'd offered you the job first."

I swallow, because this topic isn't one of my favorites even on *non*-hangover days. "She didn't really offer it to me, exactly. Just asked if I'd be interested."

"Yeah, Mac. That's pretty much what a job offer is."

"Well, call it whatever you want. It doesn't matter, because I *wasn't* interested."

"In a promotion? Why not?"

"Because not everyone likes to fit in a cookie-cutter mold. Besides, you should be glad I didn't, otherwise *you* wouldn't have a job."

"I'd have a job," he says with complete confidence. "Just not this one."

"Look, if you're worried I resent you for it, I *really* really don't," I say truthfully. "I can't imagine anything more mind-numbing than being a middle-manager. The job's all yours, okay?"

Thomas crosses his arms, and looks annoyed, but says nothing.

"No comeback?" I say, almost a little regretfully.

"None that are appropriate to say to a subordinate in the office," he grumbles, before turning away and continuing towards our meeting.

Christina's office door is open, and she waves us in.

"Mac. Thomas, morning," she says distractedly, as we sit across from her. "Sorry about the last-minute early-morning meeting invite."

"Not a problem," I lie.

I mean it *is*, but Christina is sort of my idol. Sometimes I feel bombarded by the message that a woman's life isn't complete until she finds a life partner and has kids, or at least a dog. As though it doesn't matter how great our career, how incredible our friends, or how happy we are—the message is clear: we'll be just a bit happier when we shackle ourselves to one person forever and ever.

I don't buy it, and neither, apparently, does Christina.

There is, however, a crucial difference between us: Christina doesn't just want to climb the corporate ladder, she wants to dominate it. That's not my scene.

"Okay, so before we get down to it," Christina says, placing a sheet of paper in front of both Thomas and myself. "I'm going to need you both to sign these."

I glance down, my surprise at the document bubbling to the surface. "An NDA?"

I've worked at Elodie for years now, and I've *never* been asked to sign a non-disclosure agreement. I always just sort of assumed that all the new-employee paperwork we sign before we start work covers the whole, "You can't talk about this to anyone outside the company" thing.

Thomas is carefully reading the document, because, of course he is. To be honest, I'm more of a skim-and-sign kind of gal, especially when it comes to jibberish legalese I don't understand. Not wanting to look like an idiot, I read it as well, and surprise surprise, I understand only about 15 percent of it.

Luckily, Christina spells out the important parts for us. "What we're going to talk about today doesn't go outside this building, it doesn't even go outside this *office*," she emphasizes. "To say that you two are on a very short list of need-to-know is an understatement."

Curiosity begins to smooth the edges of my hangover as Christina continues.

"You can't discuss this with your colleagues, your subordinates, not even *my* bosses. Got it?" she says, looking between us.

Thomas and I both nod. He signs his document with a pen pulled from his suit breast pocket, because Christina didn't offer us one. I lift my purse to my lap and begin to dig through it, looking for a pen of my own, since Christina's desk is the very definition of minimalist, and there's no pen cup in sight.

I rifle through the mess of my bag: a tampon, another tampon, lip gloss, a bobby pin . . . a half-eaten PowerBar that I can't remember opening, so it must be ancient . . .

But no pen.

I feel something poke against my bicep, and glance over to the pen Thomas is holding out. I accept it, because let's be real, my purse search could go on for days and still come up empty.

The pen Thomas hands me is a fancy fountain pen. Pretentious, just like its owner.

I sign my name and hand the pen back to him, and he slides the pen back into his pocket as Christina takes our NDAs. The moment she sets the documents in a folder, her face seems to light with excitement. Obviously she's *dying* to share the exclusive news.

"So." She leans towards us a little. "It just became official over the weekend. Elodie is acquiring Carbon & Shine."

"*Whoa*," I blurt out, genuinely surprised. This is one of those bits of news that outside of the biz would barely cause a ripple, but inside the biz is a bit of a tidal wave.

I'll explain. Elodie—my company—is old-school fancy. We've been around forever and are one of the oldest and best known high-end jewelry companies in the world. Imagine Elodie like you would one of those British actresses with Dame in their name: they've been around forever and keep getting better with age.

Carbon & Shine, more often known as C&S, is the Lady Gaga of diamonds. Young, edgy, and breaking all the rules. Walking into an Elodie store feels a bit like being frozen in time, and that's very intentional. We sell timeless. Classic.

Carbon & Shine has turned the jewelry retail experience upside down. Instead of sales people in conservative suits and pencil skirts and polos, you'll find tattoos and leather jackets. Instead of Sinatra softly crooning about flying to the moon, you'll hear a song you don't recognize, because the store knows what's going to be cool way before it's *actually* cool.

The only thing Elodie and C&S have in common are the massive price tags. Other than being expensive, we're basically the apples and oranges of jewelry stores.

"I know," Christina says, shaking her head. "I couldn't believe it either. It's like one minute we're all in meetings trying to figure out whether we want to try and compete with what they're doing, or differentiate ourselves even further, and the next we're . . . becoming them? Or they're becoming us?"

She shakes her head. "That's where our team comes in. None of this is public news yet, and everyone all the way to the very top is trying to keep it that way until we can control the narrative."

"They want a big reveal," Thomas says, understanding.

"Big. Massive." Christina makes a fireworks motion with her fingers. "They've brought in a superpower branding agency to spearhead the campaign, which is . . . kind of a bummer for us, we won't get to be the brains behind it, but at least we get to be a part of it, right?"

I am definitely sharing Christina's disappointment at the news of agency involvement. But I'm also not *that* surprised. It's not the first time Elodie's brought in contractors for a big campaign. But it means my role will be more execution than visionary. Someone else will decide the creative direction, and I'll more or less just be their reference for adapting the new concepts for the current website infrastructure.

Still, it's exciting news, and I can't deny there's an extra thrill from being one of the few in the know.

"I chose you specifically, Mac." Christina smiles at me. "The whole idea behind the acquisition is appealing to a different customer base, a hipper one, and that's your forte."

I grin and give a little mock bow.

"I don't doubt that Mac's the best designer for the job," Thomas says without glancing my way. "But what do you need from me?"

Christina's cheeks puff out and then she blows out a slow breath. "Honestly? I've got a feeling this is going to be a logistical nightmare. The fact that the team is so small will help a little, but there's going to be plenty of facilitation between us and Insurgence—that's the design agency. They're based in Paris, which means a whole lot of phone calls. Early-morning phone calls for you two."

Woof.

"And speaking of logistics . . ." Christina opens her desk drawer and slides two electronic key fobs across the desk, one for Thomas and myself.

"What's this?" I ask.

"Access to your new office. The higher-ups are no joke about the secrecy on this, so for the next three months, you two will be offsite at a rented workspace. It's not fancy, but the website makes it look decent, at least."

"A rented workspace," I repeat. "So like, two individual offices . . ."

"One space," Christina says distractedly, looking at her phone. "Big enough for both of you, plus access to a conference space if you need to meet with the Insurgence folks. Ah. Here we go. They found something on Fifty-Second between Ninth and Tenth for you to set up as the home base for the design portion of the project." She turns her phone around and shows a nondescript-looking brownstone. "See? Cute, right?"

It *is* cute—super cute, actually. And normally, I'd be thrilled to be able to do my job from a nondescript brownstone with a big tree outside rather than the formality of Elodie's headquarters. I love my job, but I've never loved corporate culture. Plus, this fancy office, while beautiful, isn't really my style. Give me a cramped little studio with sloped floors and drafty windows and a tree outside my window any day over a glossy skyscraper.

But I won't be *alone* in that cozy little studio, now will I? I'll be with him. For three months.

Apparently Thomas and I are on the same page for once, because he's frowning. "Are we sure that Mac and I working out of the office won't make people *more* curious about what's going on?"

"They can be curious all they want," Christina says. "But you two won't be here for them to hound for details. That's kind of the point. Plus, working remotely is hardly unusual these days. Plenty of team members have a flexible work schedule. I myself work from my living room most Fridays."

She looks between the two of us, seeming to notice for the first time that our excitement doesn't match hers. "Everything okay?"

"Totally," I say, forcing a smile. "When do we start?"

I'm not looking forward to this. At all. But my head hurts too much at the moment to fight the fact that the universe is trying to torture the two of us with each other's presence.

Plus, if I try *really* hard to look on the bright side, the shared office will make it a little easier for him and me to sync up on our maid of honor and best man duties. There's still the damn party to plan.

"Right away. You guys will take the rest of this week to transition. Mac, since Thomas is so new, I'll look to you to lead suggestions on how to divvy up your current projects among the team. You'll start in the new office next Monday, and Mac, you'll be on the secret project full time. Thomas, you'll obviously still need to support your team, but lean on me as much as you need. The merger comes first."

"Got it," he says with the same tone one might use when the dentist suggests flossing more.

He and I both pick up our key fobs, I'm pretty sure with twin inclinations to toss them in the trash, but I drop mine in my purse, him into his pocket.

"Well," Thomas says on a sigh as we head back towards my cubicle and his office on the other side of the floor. "This should be interesting."

"A euphemism if I've ever heard one," I grumble, dropping my bag onto my chair with a sigh. I glance up at him. "You think they'd notice if we just worked from home?"

"Conceding our battle of wills so soon?" he says, lifting his eyebrows.

"You know, ordinarily, that reverse psychology actually might work on me, but right now . . ." I rub at my pounding forehead. "Can we revisit our upcoming nightmare this afternoon?"

"No problem," he says, not unkindly, tapping his palm lightly atop my cubicle wall and moving away. "I'll let you get to work."

Ugh. I drop into my desk chair and close my eyes against the fluorescent lights, enjoying the relative silence since the rest of my team isn't in yet.

Eventually, I rouse myself enough to retrieve my headphones out of my desk drawer. I'm not listening to anything—my head can't handle it—but headphones are the universal visual cue for "leave me alone, I'm working."

And, surprisingly, I actually *do* get to work. It distracts me a little bit from my headache, and for all my loosey-goosey ways, the more I can get done this week, the less my team will have to take on to cover for me when I shift focus to the C&S merger on Monday.

It takes me a while to get in the zone, but I push through the mimosa-fueled brain fog until I lose myself in the holiday campaign proposal, divvying up who on the team should take point on each aspect. I let the office sort of disappear, the way it always does when I'm in what I call my CV—Creative Vortex.

Eventually, though, the damn headache pulls me out of CV, and I roll my neck to loosen the muscles.

Only then do I notice something on my desk that wasn't there before.

A triple mocha, extra whip, and a bagel.

CHAPTER EIGHT

Tuesday, September 20

◡

$\mathcal{I}$'ve lived in my current building for a few years now. And last year, I moved from the third floor to the fifth, and overlook Fifty-Sixth instead of the noisier Tenth Avenue. The apartment is bigger too. Not *big*. We're talking crowded one-bedroom. But it's a step up from the crowded studio I lived in before.

My neighborhood took some getting used to. Before this building, I lived with Collette in the East Village, with all its vibrant, trendy weirdness. Hell's Kitchen—or as city officials try to pretend it's called, *Clinton*—is vibrant and weird too, just minus the trendy.

It's grown on me though, and now I can't imagine living anywhere else. I know the nearest bagel place, the best Thai, the fastest pizza delivery, and the cheapest Greek place. Plus, I know the best park to watch cute puppies while sipping a Frappuccino on a sunny summer Sunday, and the coziest bars to tuck into on a brutal winter evening.

My apartment, too, feels like a little corner of the world that's *mine*. Which is weird, because I've never been the nesting type. Growing up in Brooklyn, Mom and I rarely stayed in the same apartment for more than a year. My mother was forever on the hunt for the best deal on rent, and I swear bargaining for concessions on new lease terms was one of her favorite activities.

And throughout all that, I'd rarely had my own bedroom. Once, in seventh grade, we'd moved in with a guy my mom was dating who'd owned a successful Park Slope deli. It had marked the first time I knew that two-bedroom apartments even existed, and for one glorious summer, I'd had a space all of my own. Joe— the deli owner—had even let me paint the walls. An electric royal purple, which had been my favorite color at the time.

Then, Mom had cheated on Joe with a bartender, who'd turned out to be married, and we'd been on our own yet again, back to the cramped one-bedrooms where I'd slept on an ugly brown pull-out couch.

I'm not complaining. I'm really not. It had simply been life as I knew it, and I actually sort of liked it. I'd been able to watch as much TV as I wanted, as late as I wanted. If I stayed up until three am drawing instead of doing homework, Mom had barely noticed, even when I came home with Cs in pretty much everything except art class.

The point is, it's taken me a while to grasp the concept of having a home, and admittedly I rent, not own, but I finally *get* it. I've finally let myself settle in, make a place of my own.

I've outgrown the electric purple, but I did paint the walls. A soft dove gray that makes me think of curling up with a cozy blanket on a rainy day. And since Manhattan life isn't exactly known for its greenery, I've tried to create some green of my own. I have a bunch of potted plants—who I've named—along the window, and my walls are covered with photos I'd taken of trees and birds during a trip to the Catskills.

And then there's the Couch. Yes, capital C, couch. It's a three-piece sectional, white, and it was ridiculously expensive. An "investment piece," the guy in the store had explained, and as with my corporate job, is one of those things that makes me feel like I'm betraying my true self. Betraying the Mac of the flea market prowess, who doesn't get attached to belongings, who has a bag under my bed that's always half-packed so I'm ready to traipse through Europe at a moment's notice. Now I also have a couch that cost way more than I make in a single month.

And yet, even with all that guilt and figurative and *literal* baggage, I can't deny that I love the couch in all its fancy, luxurious glamour.

I can still have a penchant for bad boys and naughty underwear and have nice things. Right? *Right?* Okay, yeah. I'm still working through the contradiction that I've become. It's sort of like my pre-thirtieth-birthday project.

For now, I'm focused on more basic needs: dinner.

It's Tuesday night, and I haven't gone grocery shopping in I don't *know* how long, but I open my fridge anyway. Sauvignon blanc and string cheese. Perfect.

Before I can indulge in my gourmet meal, my cell buzzes on my kitchen table, and a photo of my mom and me at a Memorial Day wine-tasting event pops up.

"Hey, Mom."

"Hey, baby! Ding dong!"

"Don't say that like I'm supposed to know what it means," I say, using my teeth to open the string cheese wrapper.

"I'm outside your front door! Are you home? Let me up! Oh, never mind—this nice boy is opening the door for me. See you in one sec!"

She hangs up in my ear and I don't even bother to sigh, because I'm pretty used to this. It's not the first time my mom's popped by unannounced. It's not even the first time this month. And I *always* like to see her, she's my only family.

It's the requests for another loan and accompanying guilt trips I could do without.

"Whoa," I say, as I open the door to a waft of vanilla. "New perfume?"

"Grant bought it for me. You like?"

"Grant. The guy from your morning call last week?"

"Hmm?" She pulls down a wine glass from my cupboard, helps herself to a glass of the wine in the fridge. "Oh, no. That was Steve. He turned out to be a *major* yawn."

She sips her wine, then sets it aside and uses both hands to sort of fluff my hair from the roots. My mom hasn't set foot in her home state of Texas since she was in her teens, and not much of her Texan beauty queen self remains. Her love of big hair though—that's stuck around.

She picks up the streak of blue hair, which I've braided today. "Love this. You get it re-blued?"

"Yup, last night." The vivid blue fades to powder blue quicker than my roots grow, so I've taken to "re-bluing" it myself with drugstore dye in between salon appointments. "So what's up?" I ask her, peeling off a string of cheese.

Mom drops onto my couch, her red hair and black leather pants looking even more vivid than usual against the white fabric. My mom is, oh, how do I put this? *Hot*. She's the kind of mom you go out with, and people ask if you're sisters and actually mean it.

I inherited her personality and her eyes, so I've been told, but not much else. She's tall to my short, willowy to my curvy, and while the current shade of red hair is enhanced, her roots are strawberry blonde to my regular blonde.

"Ugh, baby girl, you know I hate to pester, but did you have a chance to look at that VA class I sent over?"

"You love to pester," I point out.

My mom grins, though my lame attempt to dodge the question doesn't get very far.

"What do you think? Great opportunity, right? There's never been such a good time to lean into the remote workforce."

I exhale through my nose, careful to do it slowly so it doesn't sound like the sigh that it is. Honestly, I'm kind of surprised my mom's still on this. The only thing she moves through faster than men is her get-rich-quick schemes. The virtual assistant thing isn't the craziest of her ideas, just the latest. And I actually agree that it'd be good for her to have a job she could do from anywhere, especially with her nomad ways.

But an assistant? My mom can barely stay on top of the details of her own life, much less someone else's.

"So, Debbie swears by it," she continues on, referring to her longtime best friend. "Says she's making four times what she did at the salon. Anyway, look into it later, I don't want to hustle you when we should be catching up. Sit!" She pats the cushion beside her. "I want to know what's up with Mac."

I flop down and let out a tired sigh. "Nothing good."

"*Uhhhhhh* oh. Boy trouble?"

I smile a little, because Mom *always* thinks it's boy trouble.

I hesitate. "Work's kind of been a mess lately."

She picks up a lock of my hair and makes a sympathetic noise. "I don't know how you keep suffering through it. That whole corporate crap isn't *us*, baby girl."

I eat the rest of my string cheese in two large bites to keep from pointing out that without me "suffering" through the corporate crap, she'd have no one to pay her VA course, or for her latest round of Botox, or the hairstylist's conference that was going to help her "level up" her career . . .

It was hard not to notice that the hair conference I paid for took place in Vegas, and I saw a lot of pictures of her in a bikini by the pool and not a whole lot of her learning the latest balayage techniques.

"I don't love the office part of it," I admit, staring down at my wine glass. "But I do truly like my work."

"So what about it's been messy?"

I spin the stem of the glass. "The new boss."

"Right! The jerk."

"Not really. He's more . . ." How to explain? "I always just feel so inadequate around him. Like he thinks everything I do is wrong, and everything he does is perfect. And he does all of it without saying a word."

"Ohhhhhhhh yes," she says in her mother-knows-all voice. "I know those men. Very well."

I lean my head back on the cushion and look at her. "What do you do about it?"

"Leave them in my dust," she says with a small smile. "Life's too short to spend it doing things that don't make us feel good, or with *people* that don't make us feel good."

A part of me agrees with her. A big part, but this other part . . .

"But isn't getting uncomfortable every now and then a good thing? You know, like . . . personal growth? Or something?" Though, the second the words are out, I know I'm barking up the wrong tree. Mom's idea of personal growth is extensions.

"Are you remembering to meditate?" she asks, tapping my shoulder with her nail. "I promise, it'll fix all this ickiness. Or come with me to yoga. It's all about opening yourself up, and letting it all go."

I take a big sip of wine, because it's easier to try and explain to my mom that what's bothering me isn't a need to let things go.

It's more the unpleasant sensation that I don't have anything to let go of that actually *matters*.

CHAPTER NINE

Monday, September 26

⌒

*T*he following week, I open the front door to the co-working space, and it's every bit as perfect as I knew it would be from the photo Christina showed Thomas and me.

The key fob may be electronic, not unlike the keycard that gets me into my usual workplace, but that's where the similarities to the regular Elodie offices end.

There's no imposing desk with its duo of security guards carefully monitoring the keycard-controlled turnstiles.

There *is* a desk, but the guy sitting behind it has a ponytail and a smile. "Hey there! You must be Mac."

"Must be." I smile back. "But you have the advantage."

"Brian," he says. "I'm one of the two receptionists here. During regular work hours, you can find either me or Kaylee here, signing for packages, troubleshooting Wi-Fi, stocking the coffee. You know. The essentials."

Immediately, I like him. "Coffee, you say?"

Brian grins wider. "Come. I'll give you the tour."

First up is the kitchen behind the reception desk, which is cramped but well-stocked with a pod coffee machine and a fancy assortment of teas.

Brian opens a drawer, shows me a Sharpie and labels. "For if you want to bring your lunch, or threaten death upon anyone who touches your amaretto coffee creamer." He opens another drawer. "A few healthy snacks: pro-tip, avoid the birthday cake protein bar that is full of lies."

"Does anyone ever actually eat there?" I ask, at a small table leaning sharply to one side, with a chair that looks like it's made of toothpicks.

He glances over. "No. Never. Any mingling happens strictly over coffee refills, though honestly, even that's rare. Most everyone comes in with Starbucks."

"How many people is everyone?" I ask, following him up the stairs.

"There are eight rented offices, three on the second floor, three on the third, and two big offices on the top floor. All but one is rented, so that's . . . maybe twenty people? But hardly ever is everyone in the building, so it stays fairly quiet."

We walk to the third floor, and Brian points to the front of the building. "This is you. In my opinion, it's the best space in the building. High enough up to enjoy the big old maple, but not so high as to be totally blocked by it."

"It's big," I say, relieved that it's not the claustrophobic space I envisioned.

"It's technically a four-person office. But sounds like it'll just be the two of you from your company?"

I make a noncommittal noise as I lean over a desk to look

outside. He's right. A floor lower and we'd be staring at just the trunk of the beautiful maple tree, another floor up, and the leaves would block a lot of the light. At least as long as there are leaves. I smile when I realize it's early October, and we'll likely get to see the leaves on the tree change from green to gold to red, and finally fall during the three months that we're here.

It doesn't quite make up for having to share a space with Thomas, but it's a bright spot, and I'm clinging to it.

"You need anything, that's the front desk number," Brian says, holding up a business card and then setting it on the desk nearest to the door. "Though, most people just yell down the stairs. If I'm not there, Kaylee will be, at least till six, but your key gives you access to the building 24/7."

"Got it. Thanks for the help."

"Welcome!" Brian calls, as he leaves the office. I hear him whistling "Here Comes the Sun" as he makes his way back down the stairs. I wonder if he's ever not cheerful.

I boot up the work station that's already set up, as promised by Christina, and begin the process of logging in and setting up all of my programs as I like them. Since I don't have a clue what I'm supposed to be doing as it relates to the C&S project, I spend the next hour catching up on emails and chatting with Sadie who's filling me in on her most recent fling.

"Good morning."

I jump at the sound of Thomas's voice, my fingers fumbling a little in an attempt to lock my screen, even though he's standing at the doorway and too far away to read my conversation with Sadie, which was definitely not workplace appropriate.

His eyebrows go up at my clumsy obviousness, but he says

nothing as he drops his bag onto the chair and looks around. "So. This it it."

I nod, and point at the computer. "You cool if I take this one?"

"Isn't it a little late for that? But yeah, it's fine." He sits on his desk rather than his chair, fingers tapping on either side of his hip as he studies the office.

"You meet Brian?" I ask.

"Yup."

I nod. *Cool.* "So, um, I've just been doing my regular work, but if there's something else I should be focusing on . . .?"

He makes an irritated sound as he crosses his arms. "Truthfully, Mac? I feel as clueless as you on this whole thing."

I smile. "Are you supposed to admit that to your subordinate?"

"Probably not," he admits.

Thomas shrugs out of his trench coat—Burberry, I note— fancy—and hangs it on the hook by the door. He glances around the office, but doesn't seem nearly as enamored as me by the tree outside the window. In fact, I get the sense he's not seeing anything at all, that his mind is elsewhere.

"Everything okay?" I ask.

"Sure. Yes." He pulls out his chair and sits.

"Okay," I say with a shrug, starting to turn around.

"Do you remember your first week at this job?"

I pivot my chair back towards him, surprised by the question. "Yeah, of course. Why?"

He hesitates a moment. "You liked it?"

"Loved it, actually," I say automatically. "I mean, it was a little intimidating. It was only my second job out of college, and the first job had just been a temp gig at a much smaller company. But beneath all the overwhelm, I remember feeling really excited. As though I was where I'm meant to be."

He listens intently, watching me carefully, as though genuinely interested. "You still feel that way?"

This time I hesitate before responding. "Yes."

Gray eyes narrow on me, and I let out a little laugh.

"I do still love the job," I insist.

"But?"

"*But*," I add, surprised by how easy he is to talk to. "It's also not where I imagined I'd be six years later."

"Where did you think that was?"

"Anywhere else. I'm not really the long-term commitment kind of gal. Personally or professionally."

"I see. What kind of gal are you?" Thomas asks.

"I like trying new things. New people."

"And yet, you've been in the same job for six years. Had the same best friend for that time as well."

It's an annoying observation because it's true, so I lean back, cross my legs and turn the conversation around. "Your first week on the job. You like it?"

His eyes slip away from mine. He doesn't reply verbally, but he doesn't have to.

"Ah," I say lightly, understanding. "It hasn't clicked."

He tugs at the knot of his tie, then drops his hand as though it's a nervous habit he's trying to break.

"I like the company. The team. I just have this constant nagging feeling that it's not where I'm supposed to be." He drops his chin towards his chest with a laugh. "And I definitely shouldn't be sharing this with you."

"Because I'm on your team?"

He nods, and when his gaze lifts again, he seems less vulnerable, less open, as though he's tucked a part of himself away.

I'm surprised by the stab of regret, the urge to coax that part of him back out again.

Thomas looks at his watch. "We have eight minutes until nine o'clock. Let's use them to discuss Jon and Collette's party?"

"Yes!" I rub my hands together. "Are you thinking what I'm thinking?"

"Since I'm thinking you're thinking strippers—no."

"Oh, come on. It's a classic!"

"It's a cliché," he says, though he's smiling. "And Jon's made it clear he doesn't want one."

"Yeah, Collette too," I say with an exaggerated sad sigh. "It's almost enough to make me regret I'm never getting married. At least then I'd know I'd get a proper bachelorette experience once in my life."

He looks curious. "Never?"

I shake my head. "That whole *to have and to hold* thing isn't my jam. And don't look at me like that," I say, narrowing my eyes.

"Like what?"

"All skeptical. Like I can't possibly *know* what the future holds."

"Well. Can you?"

"On this? Yeah. I know what I want out of my life, and it's not to be bored to death with one guy until I die."

"You also didn't think you'd still be at Elodie for this long . . ."

I glance over my shoulder at my computer screen. "Four minutes until we shift conversation to work . . ."

"Right. Right. So the party. Any ideas?" he asks.

"Actually . . . yes. What about Vermont?" I say.

He blinks. "Vermont?"

"Well, neither of them are Vegas people, so that's out. Collette's not into the beach, so that rules out the Hamptons. And Collette loves all things fall—it's why she chose an October wedding date. I found this little resort up in Vermont that's supposedly great for groups. There's a spa on-site for the girls. Whisky-tasting and wine-tasting are nearby. There's even a boozy foliage tour, where you can rent a fancy bus and they drive you around and let you sip Champagne while taking in the changing leaves."

"Too girly?" I prompt when he doesn't say anything. "Because the resort also has a game room you can rent, the guys could do like a poker night—"

"No, that actually sounds pretty great," he says.

"Don't get too impressed," I say. "Aside from calling to see if they had room for us, the extent of my planning so far is creeping on their Instagram."

Thomas reaches into his bag and pulls out a sleek black notebook, then the ever-present fountain pen out of his suit.

"Name of the place?" he says, opening the book.

"The Chestnut Inn. Cute, right?"

He makes a noncommittal noise as he writes, then shuts the notebook.

"I'll make sure we get the rooms reserved. For the rest of it, I'll come up with a project plan by the weekend."

"Do you ever *not* have a plan?" I ask, genuinely curious.

He caps his pen and considers my question in all seriousness. "Rarely. Do you ever *have* a plan?"

"Rarely."

"The way you like it." He says it as a statement, not a question.

"You're a quick learner, Decker, I'll give you that." I push back my chair and stand. "Coffee?"

"Sure, thanks."

"Splash of milk, right? And don't look so surprised," I say, noting his expression. "I listen."

He'd mentioned his coffee preference that morning I'd had the hangover.

"And you take yours with sugar, cream, and the tiniest splash of coffee."

I frown down at him on my way out of the office. "How do you know that?"

He gives me a cocky grin. "I saw you in the kitchen a couple times last week. I watch."

"Yikes. Creepy, boss. Very, very creepy."

But also? A little flattering too.

CHAPTER TEN

Monday, September 26

⤳

*T*he rest of the morning passes with surprising ease between us. Thomas spends most of it on the phone, coordinating next steps with the agency and senior leadership, while I go back and forth with Stevie and Sadie on the landing page for the spring campaign until I get orders on what to do next.

At noon, I turn off my go-to work playlist (eighties rock anthems) and pull off my headphones. I'm about to ask if Thomas wants to grab lunch—in the name of workplace camaraderie, of course—but Thomas has other plans because he tells me he'll see me in an hour, and leaves.

Oh. Okay then. I try *really* hard not to wonder if he's gone off to meet Anna for some sort of midday tryst. I try, and fail, because now it's all I can think about. Him, with her, and . . .

It bothers me way more than it should, but I'm pretty sure that's only because I've been going through a dry spell myself. I beat Thomas back to the office and spend the last few minutes of my lunch break on TapThat. I haven't used the dating app much at all since the disastrous evening where I met Thomas, and I'm feeling a little itchy from lack of . . . companionship.

But just because I like casual doesn't mean I'm not particular, and none of the guys the app is suggesting do it for me. I close the app without tapping anyone, feeling fussy and frustrated. Maybe I'm overthinking it, maybe I should just . . .

I unlock my phone again, and before I can talk myself out of it, I text Kris Powers.

Drinks tonight? You owe me.

I add a kissy face to soften it, but seriously—he *does* owe me.

Not only for standing me up, but also because technically this is his fault that things between Thomas and myself are so strange. Had Kris shown up that night at Smoke & Baron, I'd never have rejected Thomas, he'd never have had to see me reject him. In fact, I doubt we would have noticed each other at all. He'd just be some guy drinking a martini, sitting next to a couple on a date.

Yeah, yeah, Thomas would still be my boss and Jon's brother, but we'd have been able to navigate those with a lot less awkwardness had it not been for The Night.

Like I said: Kris's fault.

"Mackenzie. You can't be serious."

I whirl around and make a squeak of outrage when I see Thomas standing right behind me, unabashedly looking over my shoulder at the message I've just sent.

"What the hell! Creep, much!"

"Sorry."

I narrow my eyes. "No, you're not."

"This is the guy that stood you up?" He bends down to get a closer look.

"He apologized," I say defensively. It had been a lame apology, I believe the exact text had been **Shit, sorry babe**. And it had come two days late. But still, an apology was an apology.

The look Thomas gives me is downright pitying, and it pisses me off. Holding his gaze, I pick up my headphones and slowly, purposefully put them in my ears. *Go away.*

Thomas gets the hint, returning to his own desk. We both get back to our work, though the mood in our shared office feels a touch more acrimonious than it had been during the morning hours.

Even when I break to pee and then take a walk around the block to stretch my legs, we don't acknowledge each other's presence.

Just before four, he scoots his chair towards mine and taps my elbow none-too-gently. "Hey. I just got a meeting invite for the kickoff call with Insurgence tomorrow morning. Got a minute to prep?"

"You're the boss." I turn off Pat Benatar. "How early tomorrow morning?"

Thomas runs a tongue along his teeth. "You're not going to like it."

I sigh. "There are very few things I hate about Paris, but the six-hour time difference is one of them."

"The meeting's at seven—" he says over my groan. "But I did ask that we aim for eight or later in the future. We'll see how it goes."

"You're one of *them*, aren't you?" I accuse. "One of those terrible morning people? I bet you are. You look like one."

"Guilty. I take it you are not?"

"Nope. Committed night owl as long as I can remember. So don't expect charming Mac at seven am."

"Have I even met charming Mac?"

I narrow my eyes.

"How about this?" he says with a slight smile. "There's no way to get around the time difference between here and Paris. But outside of the necessary conference calls, you can make your own schedule. I don't care if the work gets done at nine am or three am as long as it gets done."

"Wow. Thanks," I say, a little surprised. Elodie has become increasingly flexible in the past couple of years about where we work, but they're pretty old-school in the nine-to-five thing. I wouldn't have expected Mr. Rulebook to be the first boss to fully respect that not everyone works the same way, at the same time.

"No prob," he replies. "I'm a little jealous, actually. Not about the three am thing, but that your job in all this will have such a clear deliverable."

"Yours doesn't?"

"I'm a middle manager," he says with a slight smile, as though this explains everything.

"Yeah, what even *is* that?" I joke. I mean, I know, but I don't really know. It's part of the reason I had balked when Christina had suggested I might want to step into those shoes.

"Exactly," he says with a quiet, self-deprecating laugh.

"No, I'm really asking," I say curiously. "I mean, I've had a couple of bosses in your role before you, but mostly they were just there for performance reviews and if I needed to request time off. I've never been clear on what they actually did with their time. No offense," I add quickly, realizing I'm being perhaps a bit too familiar. And borderline insulting.

He lifts a shoulder. "It depends on the day. The quarter. There are performance reviews, as you've said, which for us, take a lot longer than the actual review itself. You're copied in on just about every email, which, with a team of eleven, means I basically live in my inbox. You handle disagreements, frustrations. You field requests from other departments who want to make demands on your team's time to save their own. You sit through a lot of conference calls in which your attendance is required, but not your opinion."

"So, it's exactly what you wanted to be when you grew up?"

He laughs, and it's a nice laugh. Low and surprised. "Yeah. Sure."

"What *did* you want to be when you grew up?"

"You first."

"Easy," I say without hesitating. "Rock star. Obviously."

"Obviously."

"I had backup plans though," I say. "I'm very reasonable like that. If the rock star thing didn't work out, I was going to be in the NBA. Not WNBA, mind you. NBA. I was quite clear on that distinction."

He tilts his head. "How tall are you?"

"Five two. Why do you ask?" I say, twirling my hair.

Thomas smiles. "No reason. Continue."

"Right, so rock star, then pro basketball. Let's see what else was on the list? Manicurist, though only if science invented nail polish that dried instantly. Oh, and I wanted to be Secretary of State for a while."

"That's specific . . ."

"President would have been way too much pressure," I continue. "Oh! I wanted to be a lobsterman for a while. My mom dated a guy who took us to Maine to visit his family. I tasted my first lobster roll, went to heaven, and decided to go straight to the source."

I think some more. "Okay, I think that's my complete list."

"Oh, is that all?"

"Your turn," I persist.

Thomas's smile is a little sad. "You put me to shame. I can't remember what I wanted to be. I don't know that I wanted to be *anything*."

I see now, why his smile was sad. Because it *is* sad.

"Maybe you just haven't figured it out yet," I say gently. "Or maybe, you know . . . this is it." I gesture at his desk and computer set-up.

"Hmm. Maybe." He looks out the window beyond my shoulder for a moment. "I just realized, somewhere over the years, we've switched roles."

"How so?"

He looks back at me. "*You* were the one with the plan as a child. I had none. Now I plan everything, and you . . ."

"Wing it," I finish for him. "So, if you plan everything, what's next for you, career-wise?"

"I move up. I was a manager. Now I'm a senior manager. Next, I'll be a director. Then senior director. And so on."

Yuck. Still, different strokes and all that . . .

"Well, now see," I say, with encouragement, because *my* awful doesn't have to be *his* awful. "You *do* know what you want!"

"I didn't say I knew what I wanted. Just that I had a *plan*."

"Okay, I'm confused. Aren't those the same things?"

He frowns and looks away. "No. No, apparently they are not."

CHAPTER ELEVEN

Monday Night, September 26

∾

I wouldn't go so far as to say that Collette's a bridezilla, but she *is* Collette, which means when she turns her attention to something big, like say, her wedding, it takes up 100 percent of her focus.

Which is why I've been trying to buffer her from my latest drama, but I can't take it anymore. I *need* my best friend to weigh in on the Thomas thing. And so I finally fill Collette in on every last painful detail of the Thomas–Mac saga.

"Oh my *god*, so he actually saw as you rejected him?" Collette's eyes are wide, her expression half-fascinated, half-horrified.

"Yup." I take a huge bite of lasagna and wash it down with a sip of chianti. "He had a front row seat."

Collette is shaking her head as she adds another heap of salad to her plate. She's healthy like that. "Okay, that's one of those things that only happens in movies."

"Right? Horror movies," I clarify. "Especially when you factor in the fact that I saw him again, not once, but *twice*, in two different contexts."

"Well. At least he didn't turn out to be some asshole," my best friend says.

I give her a dark look.

"What! Thomas is a totally nice guy."

"You *have* to say that. He's going to be your brother-in-law."

"True, but he *really* is sweet. He's like a slightly shyer version of Jon."

"Who's shyer than me?" Collette's fiancé asks, coming out of the bathroom, hair still damp from his post-workout shower.

He drops on the couch beside Collette and helps himself to a crouton from her plate, and she kisses his cheek.

It's a spontaneous, domestic kind of moment and I unabashedly study it as I lick tomato sauce off my fork. I've never wanted that kind of comfortable familiarity. Not because there's anything wrong with it, it just hasn't really appealed. When it comes to spending time with guys, I'm more of a "Let's have a good time, the wilder the better, then retreat back to our respective lives" kind of gal.

But I can't deny that Collette and Jon make it look good. Damn good.

"Thomas," Collette says, pointing her wine glass at me. "I was just telling Mac how great he is."

"I'm biased, but yep," Jon says, pouring himself a glass of wine. "He's a good dude. Granted, I've never had him as a boss."

"They met *before* that," Collette tells him gleefully. "Get this, he came up on her dating app. And she rejected him as he was sitting *right next to her.*"

"Hold up." I wave my fork to clarify. "That makes me sound cruel. You're forgetting a crucial clarification. I didn't *know* he was sitting right next to me. It was the universe being a little bitch at both our expenses."

"Wait, are you serious? That actually happened?" Jon asks, staring at me, and it's hard not to notice how much he resembles Thomas. Jon's eyes are a warmer blue, his features slightly broader, a touch softer, but there's no mistaking they're brothers.

"He would have told me about that," Jon says, then reconsiders. "Actually, no, he wouldn't have."

"Really?" Collette asks Jon, surprised. "I thought you guys were close."

"We are, as far as adult brothers go. But Thomas has never . . . he doesn't talk about that stuff."

"By stuff, you mean *girls*?" I say, drawing out the word like a little kid scandalized by the opposite sex.

Jon grins. "Exactly. He's always been private about that stuff, even more so after Janie."

"Who's Janie?" Collette asks, and thank goodness she does, because I'm dying to know.

"Eh." Jon looks hesitant, glancing at me, clearly regretting bringing up a woman from his brother's past in front of me.

"I'm a vault," I say, crossing my heart. "I won't mention her."

He narrows his eyes slightly. Fair. I am totally not a vault, and I am not even remotely good at keeping secrets.

Jon sighs and relents anyway. "She was this girl he was seeing a couple of years ago. We all thought they were going to get married. Thomas had already been talking rings. Then her ex showed up, some hotshot consultant who'd broken up with her when he moved to London, but then came back for her."

"Oh, poor Thomas," Collette said.

Jon nods. "I think it gutted him a little. It would anyone."

"This Anna girl seems to be perfect for him though," Collette says, swiping at a bit of lasagna sauce on her chin with her napkin.

I feel a little stab of . . . something.

"True," Jon agrees. "She reminds me a little of Janie, actually. Same vibe."

Sure, if you call *boring* a vibe.

It's a nasty little thought that comes out of nowhere, and is brutally unfair. I don't know Anna, I've never even met this Janie.

The thought lingers anyway.

"Small world though," Jon is saying, looking at me. "You and he crossing paths so often."

"Tell me about it," I say around a mouthful of food.

My tone must betray that I think the situation is a lot more dire than merely "small world," because Collette gives me a *be nice* look, and Jon looks surprised. "You don't like Thomas?"

Crap. "No! I mean yes. Of course I do." I scramble, setting my plate aside. "It's just . . . I think both he and I would have preferred our first meeting to also be our last. Now we're working together five days a week, and then there's your guys' party, and then the wedding . . ."

And I haven't even let myself think about the fact that for as long as Collette and I are friends, and Thomas and Jon are brothers, we're always going to be a little part of each other's lives.

So . . . *forever.* I can't even.

"Oh, speaking of the party—" Jon breaks off when Collette jabs an elbow into his side and glares at him.

"Uh oh," I say, my gaze moving between them.

Collette sighs. "Okay, so, Jon and I spent some time earlier this week putting together a list of people we want to invite."

"And . . . there's murder in the mix?" I joke. "Why the face?"

"Well, it's just . . ." Collette twirls a lock of her hair in a gesture I know means she's nervous. "Almost everyone on the list is either married, or in a pretty serious relationship, so we were kind of thinking of inviting plus-ones."

"Oh. Jeez, is that all? I've hung out with you guys' friends before, I never mind being the fifth wheel, or eleventh wheel, or whatever."

"See, that's exactly what we told him!" Jon says, relieved. "That you'd be totally cool with it."

I narrow my eyes. "Him?"

"Thomas thought it would be a jerk move to make the party a couples thing, when the maid of honor and co-coordinator is single. He didn't want you to feel left out."

A sharp emotion jabs me right in the throat, and I'm pretty sure it's rage.

Collette is watching me with best-friend levels of wariness. She knows me well enough to know that I loathe anything resembling pity, especially when it relates to my lifestyle.

My *chosen* lifestyle. My *choice*.

How dare that asshole presume that I'm some sort of sad, single girl to be pitied and planned around! How dare . . .

My gaze skirts over to Jon, who looks a little confused by what I imagine is my pissed expression. He and Collette are holding hands now, and I catch the way her knuckles tense for a split-second, and I know I've just witnessed a silent couple conversation. The hand squeeze that is meant to soothe, or tell him to stand down or . . .

I actually have no idea, because I've never been in one of those: a relationship that communicates in touch that doesn't have to do with hooking up.

It's a reminder, though, that this party isn't about me, or Thomas, or the fact that I hate his high-handed, condescending interference. This is about my best friend and her future husband, who is also my friend.

It's not Jon's fault his brother's an ass.

I force a smile. "Seriously, you guys. A couples thing sounds great, and it makes the most sense, honestly. I think you guys are going to love what Thomas and I have planned."

"Awesome!" Jon says, grinning. "Mac. You are seriously cool."

I smile back and take a sip of my wine. I *am* cool. But that doesn't mean Thomas Decker and I aren't going to have a few words.

~~

When I leave Jon and Collette's house a little while later, I'm feeling distinctly out of sorts for a whole jumble of reasons.

I thought I'd totally accepted the fact that she's getting married, and I'm happy for her—for them—I really truly am.

But I'm also realizing that gone are the nights that Collette and I would spend all night talking or watching movies.

She's part of a *we* now, and I'm still an I.

And happy as I am with that, I'd be lying if I didn't admit that the more friends jump on the *we* train, the more I'm aware of something that feels a bit like loneliness.

I frown when I realize the train of my thoughts comes *awfully* close to proving Thomas right: That sometimes being the only

single person sucks. It's a relatively new realization for me, and it's
a little jarring that this realization has been handed to me via a
man that I don't even like.

Just when I thought he and I were sort of making progress
towards tolerating each other, he has to go and piss me off all over
again.

I reach into my bag to pull out my phone to make sure I have
enough money on my MetroCard app; I'm forever not realizing
how low it is until I fail to get through the turnstile with a half-
dozen people behind me.

I have a message from Kris Powers.

**Babe. My place? You're right, I have some things to make up
to you . . .**

Huh.

It's a booty call if I've ever seen one, and my brain tells me to go
for it. That a fun fling with a hunky trainer is exactly what I need
right now. Not only because it's been a while, but because it feels
a little vindictive, like a middle finger to Thomas, even if he never
knows about it.

It may be what I need.

But for some stupid reason, it's not what I want, and I know
exactly who to blame for my current mood.

Thomas gave his cell number to all of his team his first day on
the job, telling us he was available any time, for any thing.

I'm pretty sure this wasn't what he had in mind, but I *really*
don't give a shit.

**Did you tell your brother and Collette I was the saddest single
girl in all the land?**

I fire off the message and glare at the screen, willing him to respond now, and the universe must have picked up my anger, because he actually does.

Yes, Mac. I said that. Those exact words. How eerie to be quoted verbatim.

Normally I'd be impressed by how clearly he manages to convey sarcasm via the written word, but I'm too irritated to compliment him.

Me: **Stay out of my personal life. Just because you and perfect Anna went from strangers to plus-1 status doesn't mean the rest of us are equally desperate.**

Thomas: **I'M desperate?! Which of us is throwing ourselves at a guy who CLEARLY isn't interested? Tell me, Mac, how IS Mr. Personal Trainer?**

The nerve!

I'll be sure and let you know tomorrow morning! I'm headed over there right now!

After only a moment's hesitation, I send the eggplant emoji as well. Just in case Thomas missed my meaning.

I wait. And wait.

Nothing.

Just as I'm about to put my phone away, it buzzes again, and I almost drop it in my haste to get it.

Only, it isn't Thomas. It's Kris again, this time with his address.

He lives downtown, just a few blocks from Collette and Jon. I can actually walk from here!

Perfect.

A minute later, I find myself getting on the train.

The *uptown* train.

Away from my booty call.

I drop onto a hard, empty seat and stare out the window, trying to identify what's wrong with me.

By the time I get back to my apartment, I haven't figured out the what.

But I'm pretty clear on the who.

CHAPTER TWELVE

Tuesday Morning, September 27

⌒

*T*o say that the following morning is tense between Thomas and myself would be an understatement. Between the angry text exchange last night, the fact that I had to wake up at 5:30 to be showered and primped in time for this stupid seven am meeting, the mood in the office can best be described as *simmering*.

Our "Morning"'s are terse and perfunctory, and we don't say much more than that, even as I pull my chair over to his so we can share a camera for the conference call.

Which, actually? Turns out to go pretty well.

The Insurgence team is friendly and excited, and most surprising of all, effusive in their praise. Christina must have sent over my portfolio, because they're going on and on about my work, and style, and how it's exactly the direction they have in mind for the Elodie/C&S campaign.

After the month I've been having, I don't mind the praise one little bit, and it's made all the sweeter by the fact that Thomas has to sit right next to me and hear every word of it.

He's mostly quiet in the meeting, speaking eloquently when necessary, but mainly just taking notes in his stupid little notebook. When the leader of the Insurgence team calls me a visionary, I really want to tell him to write *that* down.

The meeting takes the full scheduled hour, but when it ends, I'm in a better mood than when I started.

In addition to the significant boost to my ego, the agency made it pretty clear that they have no interest in micromanaging me. They'll do print media, social media, but it'll be up to me to decide how to bring the theme—*fusion*—to life on Elodie's website.

It's also been decided that in order for me to spend most of my time on the creative stuff, all the boring, facilitation crap and meetings will go through Thomas. That part isn't quite as great, but it's also kind of what I expected.

"That went well," I say as he ends the chat and leans back in his chair.

"Yes."

"What do you think of the theme?"

"I think it doesn't matter what I think, I'm just supposed to do as I'm told," he says tersely. "Did you finish your expense report yet?"

So it's going to be like that. "No, sir. Not yet, sir. But I'll get right to work on it. Sir."

He doesn't even bother to respond.

I drag my chair back to my desk and get to work on the damn expense report. It's not technically due until the end of the month, so I have a few days, and I'm seriously tempted to turn it in at the very last second just to be a pain.

But something tells me poking the bear is not the right strategy right now, and I hate administrative tasks like this, so I'm eager to get it off my plate. I'm pushing my way through the tedium when I feel something light hit me on the back of my arm. I glance down and see a wadded-up piece of paper. Thomas has thrown it at me, and the fact that he's resorted to such childish behavior helps lifts my spirit.

I pull my left earbud out to see what he wants, my tone clipped. "What."

"I'm hungry. I'm going to grab an early lunch. You want me to bring you anything?"

I'm surprised by the offer, and also crazy-grateful for it. Given the early morning, I didn't have time to grab breakfast. Who am I kidding? I never do.

"Sure," I say a little warily. "Whatever you're having is fine."

"Burrito?"

My stomach rumbles in approval, and I reach for my wallet.

"Text me your order," he says curtly, pulling on his jacket and leaving our little office. "You can pay me back later."

Alright. So we haven't exactly achieved *best friends!* status, but at least we're on speaking terms.

As requested, I text him my order: chicken burrito, no beans, extra guac, extra cheese, and a Diet Coke.

I've learned the hard way that burritos aren't "eat at the expensive keyboard" friendly, but neither do I want to sit at that sad little table in the kitchen. The office space came with a little wheeled filing cabinet under the desk that we're never going to use, because it's not the 1970s.

There. Makeshift table.

After a moment's hesitation, I wheel Thomas's chair to the

opposite side. He made the first move in being civil, if not exactly friendly, by picking up food. Here's my counter attempt.

Thomas returns in record time, probably because he beat the lunch rush, and hesitates a moment when he sees my table set-up, but when I lift my eyebrows in silent challenge, he takes a seat.

We unwrap our food, peeling back foil, popping soda can tabs, and tearing open plastic utensil bags, all without saying a word. And for some reason, the whole situation reminds me of an old-fashioned standoff in a Wild West town, only with burritos instead of pistols. The visual makes me laugh.

"What?" He takes a bite of burrito and glares at me.

"Nothing." Then I change my mind and tell him anyway about our imaginary burrito duel.

Thomas chews and says nothing, and my smile fades a little that my peace offering is being shut down. Then he whistles a tune, that's so spot-on Western that I laugh again.

His smile is more reluctant, but definitely present.

"So, what kind of burrito guy are you?" I ask, after taking a bite and swallowing.

"I'm sorry?" Thomas wipes his mouth.

I point with my burrito to his. "Steak? Chicken? Veggie?"

"Ah. Chorizo. Habanero salsa, and I tell them not to be shy with it."

"Habanero," I repeat. "The super-hot one?"

He meets my eyes. "You sound surprised."

"Well." I chew a bite methodically and take a sip of my soda. "Yes. I confess I had you pegged more as a . . ."

He lifts his eyebrows in question.

"I didn't think you'd go for spicy," I admit.

Thomas takes his time, setting down his burrito, taking a sip of his sparkling water, as he leans forward and captures my gaze. "I like it hot."

I freeze in place. Something about the way he says it, the way he's looking at me, makes me think he's not talking about salsa. And even more surprising than this unexpected side of Thomas is my reaction.

Now *I* feel suspiciously hot, and it has nothing to do with my salsa, which is mild.

Then I see it. Just the tiniest of smirks that he covers quickly, but not quickly enough. He knew exactly what he was doing.

I keep my features schooled in indifference, because I don't even want to think about the fact that I was temporarily very attracted to him, much less talk about it.

"So. What did you think of the call this morning?" I ask.

He shakes his head. "It's our lunch break, let's not talk about work. Did you see my note about the room block at the Vermont hotel? We're all good."

"Right, yep. Thanks for taking care of that." I make a confused face. "Though, I'm a little unclear. As the lone single girl, what should I do? Do I announce that when I book? Wear a scarlet S for Single? Or Sad? I just hope they know to put me on the opposite side of the building from all the happy couples so I don't drag down the mood. Better yet, I think there's a barn on the property. Perhaps I sleep there."

"I get it, Mac," he says, using a napkin to wipe the corner of his mouth. "I should have stayed out of your business. I told you I was sorry about that."

I burst out laughing. "No, you did not!"

His smile is crooked. "I didn't apologize?"

"Not even close."

"Ah. Well." Thomas picks up his burrito again. "I *do* apologize. I meant well. When Jon and Collette mentioned making it a couples weekend, I thought of . . ."

"Sad, single me."

He sighs and sets his burrito down. "I was thinking more that odd numbers are sometimes tricky."

"That is so *you* to think that. But rest assured, Mr. Even Numbers. Maybe I'm planning on bringing someone."

His eyes flash with . . . something. "V-cut?"

I shrug.

He starts to pick up his food again, then stops. "How was last night? He turn out to be the love of your life?"

"Not all of us declare eternal love after three dates."

"I take it that's an unsubtle dig at my relationship with Anna, and the fact that I brought her to Jon's engagement party?"

"I really didn't mean it to be a dig," I say honestly. "You and I just approach things differently. There's nothing wrong with that."

"As I recall, we were *both* on the same dating app."

"And look how well that went," I say. Then I frown. "Actually, why *were* you on that app?" I ask, because it's been bothering me, especially now that I know he was almost going to marry that Janie woman. "I mean, you know that TapThat is more about . . ."

"Sex."

I shift in my chair. "Right. Yeah."

He blows out a breath. "Off the record? Not as your boss?"

I nod, and he leans forward. "I have sex, Mac. And I like it."

I choke on a piece of rice.

He leans back once more, way more nonchalant about the conversation than me, which is jarring. *I'm* supposed to be the cool one!

"The difference is," he continues, "I know that sex can be better with the right person, not just *any* person."

My brain scrambles, trying to find a witty, succinct counterargument, to tell him he's wrong, that *my* way is infinitely hotter because you get variety and excitement and . . .

The longer he holds my gaze, his eyes no longer seeming as cold as they did when we first met, the more my thoughts seem to scatter. I'm struggling to remember all the reasons I stay single, to form all the arguments against being with just one person.

Most confusing at all, I'm fighting to remember all the reasons why he wasn't my type.

CHAPTER THIRTEEN

Tuesday Evening, September 27

*have no idea how this happened. None.

One minute I was packing up for the day, debating whether to go to the store as planned to pick up something nutritious for dinner or order a pizza, extra cheese.

The next, Thomas is asking if I want to get together that evening to plan out the itinerary for Jon and Collette's weekend.

And then, not only am I saying yes, *I'm inviting him over.*

Yes. That's right.

I invited Thomas Decker, my boss and my sort-of enemy *to my apartment.*

Tonight.

And he said yes.

Now, this is going to shock nobody, but my apartment isn't exactly set up to be "company-ready" at a moment's notice. Which means I've spent the past hour as a human tornado, whirling around the apartment, putting away shoes, frantically cleaning out all stray hair strands from the bathroom, all while trying to identify the source of a funky smell.

(The culprit: A rogue fried rice container under the sink, and nothing that a quick run to the trash and spritz of air freshener can't handle.)

And *just* as I think I have a grip on the entire situation, the unthinkable happens.

"Baby girl!"

Great. My mother.

The woman's like a ninja at getting into my building, and I return her hug in resignation. Her perfume is different this time, more floral. Another gift from another boyfriend, no doubt.

"Hi. What are you doing here?" I check in the hallway to make sure Thomas hasn't followed her up. "Can I call you tomorrow? My boss is coming over any minute."

She halts her scan of my fridge contents. "Your *boss*? Comes to your house?"

"Yeah, I know. I don't really understand it either."

I continue to hold the front door open, hoping she'll get the hint and leave. Instead, she sniffs the air. "It smells good in here. Different."

"It's called clean."

"Huh. Well, honey, don't rush me out! I'll just say a quick hi to . . . her?" she says, pouring herself a bit of wine from an open bottle that I'm pretty sure is quite old, but she doesn't seem to mind.

"Him."

My mom sighs. "I was afraid of that. Listen, baby girl. I know what's going on here, and I get it. Men in power positions are delicious. But take it from me, that kind of power dynamic is sexy at first, but will blow up in your face."

It's a rare moment when my mother decides to be, well, motherly, and I'd be touched if her warning wasn't so entirely misplaced.

"Trust me, he is so not interested in me like that."

Mom takes affront. "Why not? You're smart and strong and sexy."

I lift my hand. "Please don't call me sexy. It's weird."

"It's *true*. And why would he be coming over if not to get in your pants? Have I taught you nothing about men?"

Not really, no.

"Because in addition to being my boss, he's Collette's fiancé's brother, and we're planning the bachelor party together."

"Ooh. Strippers?"

"Sadly, no. I'll fill you in tomorrow." I make a sweeping gesture with my arm out the door. *You've got to go.*

She downs the rest of her wine in a single gulp. "Fine, fine. I'll leave. But only if you tell me why you think this man wouldn't be interested in my baby girl. Didn't I raise you to be confident about your appeal?"

"Yes, and you also taught me to be realistic about my prospects and compatibility. He's a *marrying* guy, Mom."

"Oh." She puts a hand over her chest, horrified. "Say no more."

"Exactly," I say with feeling. "Now, would you please—"

"Good evening."

I groan aloud at the calm, masculine voice, knowing even before I turn that I'm going to find Thomas standing there.

Even still, I do a double-take, because this is not a Thomas I'm familiar with. Instead of a suit, he's wearing jeans and a thin gray v-neck sweater layered over a black T-shirt. He's still wearing fancy shoes, some sort of loafer, and he's still a far cry from my usual type with Chucks and tats and stubble, but my mouth is absurdly dry for some reason.

His cool eyes light on mine for a moment before shifting towards my mother. "Hi. I'm Thomas Decker."

"The boss who wants to get married," my mom says, coming forward and extending her hand with the grace of a southern debutante. "I'm the mother."

Thomas surprises me by taking her extended hand without hesitation, raising it to his lips gallantly, and kissing the back of it.

For a horrible, confusing moment, I'm jealous of my own mother. I want her hand to be my hand. No, I want her hand to be my—

Good god, Mac. It's Thomas.

But this casual version of him, with the tight-fitting sweater that shows the faintest outline of biceps I definitely did not see coming, it makes me a little . . . *something*

"Hello, The Mother," he says, in the clipped tone that is becoming more and more appealing the more I hear it. "I regretfully must admit that yes, I am in fact one of those dreadful marrying types."

"Oh, not *dreadful*," Mom backpedals enthusiastically. "It's just not the Austin women way."

"I've heard that." He cuts a gaze my way, and I feel the eye contact in all sorts of tingly ways.

Mom picks up her wine glass and makes some sort of murmuring noise that translates pretty clearly to *I knew it.*

"So, Thomas. How old are you?"

"*Ohhhhkay*, and that is where we say goodbye, Mom." I plant a hand on her back and none-too-gently maneuver her out the door.

She surprisingly lets me, though her attention is still on Thomas. "Lovely to meet you, Mr. Bossman."

"And you as well, Mac's mother."

"Please, call me Annette."

"He won't be calling you anything," I say, starting to close the door. "You two will never meet again, and we will never speak of this night."

She gives me another knowing glance. *Mmm hmm.* "Bye, baby girl!" she calls, already heading down the hallway.

I shut the door to my apartment, slumping against it as I look up.

"Actually, yeah. How old are you?" I ask.

He smiles. "Thirty-one."

"Huh. I thought you were older." I pick up my mom's wine glass and finish the contents.

"Thanks? Sorry to let myself in. The front door of your building doesn't close all the way."

"I know. My mom takes full advantage of that fact regularly. Drink?"

I grab two beers out of the fridge, pop the top off both, and hand him one.

"Sorry about her," I say, after taking a swig.

"Don't be. She was . . . enlightening."

"Do I even want to know what that's supposed to mean?" I ask warily, flopping on my couch.

Thomas smiles. "So your aversion to committed relationships is in your blood, huh?"

He sits on the other side of the couch, and it's not as odd as it should be, having Thomas Decker in my home, on my couch, drinking my beer, meeting my mother . . .

"I think it was more nurture than nature," I say, surprising myself by answering his question. "I grew up without a dad, which I'm sure was part of it, but it was more that she never tried to soften that absence for me, because she didn't think that it *was* an absence. For as long as I can remember, men came and went from her life—our life—but there was never any promise of permanency, or even desire for it, really. In fact, I think it sort of sticks in her craw that I've had the same job at Elodie as long as I have. Like it's a betrayal of the Austin woman's essence, or something."

I glance over at him, half expecting judginess, or maybe even pity, but he looks simply thoughtful.

"Different from your upbringing, I'm guessing?" I prod.

"Very. My parents met in their early twenties, married in their mid-twenties, and they've never been shy or embarrassed about declaring themselves soulmates, even to a trio of scandalized teenage sons."

"And you want what they have," I say. "Stability."

"I do. Just as you want what your mother has."

"*Lack* of stability?"

He sips his beer. "I was going to say spontaneity."

"Which is a synonym for lack of stability."

"Hmm." He considers. "Fun? I think you and your mom seek fun. How's that?"

I both watch and listen closely for mocking, but I find none. I sit up a little straighter and scoot closer, filled with sudden intensity, a sudden need for reassurance or soothing or . . . something.

"What if . . . what if that's not enough?" I blurt it out, and wish immediately I could take it back.

A line appears between Thomas's thick, serious brows. "What do you mean?"

I look down at my beer, peel at the label, shaking my head quickly. "Nothing. It's stupid."

"No. Tell me."

I look up, and realize I'm not the only one who's closed some of the space between us. He seems to have moved closer as well. And though he's leaning forward, arms on his knees, beer dangling casually from his fingers, his face is turned towards me. All of his attention is on me, and there's nothing casual about it.

I take a deep breath as I set my beer on the coffee table. "What if I'm missing out on something?"

Thomas continues to gaze at me steadily, patiently waiting for me to finish my thought, but I don't even know what my thought is, or where it's coming from. And I definitely don't know why I'm telling *him*.

"Missing out on . . .?" he prompts softly.

"I don't know." I close my eyes and shake my head and laugh. "Seriously, forget it. I think just seeing you and my mom in the same space. Worlds colliding and all that." I mash my fingers together in an explosion, then pick up my beer again.

Thomas sets his own beer on the table, barely touched, and clasps his hands. He stares down at his fingers, linked between his knees, looking deep in thought. Finally, he looks over at me again. "You know, I'm almost always thinking and acting with Future Thomas in mind."

"Yes. I've noticed." I smile.

He smiles back, but it's distracted. When he continues, his voice is lower. "But lately I've been wondering if I haven't missed out on something pretty fantastic by not living in the moment. By not trusting instinct over plans. Doing things *your* way."

A strange buzzy feeling has taken over me, surrounded me. I'm listening to what he's saying, I am, but more than I hear it, I *feel* it.

I don't know if I've moved even closer, or if he has, or if I'm just now aware of his proximity, or the fact that we're alone, or that he was surprisingly nice to my mother.

That he's so nice to me . . .

But suddenly I'm uncomfortably aware of him. Of those eyes, his mouth, his nearness . . .

His words replay in my mind:

I've been wondering if I haven't missed out on something pretty fantastic by not living in the moment.

Is he talking about . . . *us?*

And just like that, all my maudlin musings about what I'm missing out on fade away, and there's only right now, me and him, living in the moment.

I lean in a little more, moth to a flame, pulled to him against all reason.

"Thomas." My voice is a whisper, confused. Frustrated. Wanting.

I lean forward without meaning to, my gaze drops to his mouth.

His drops to mine too, I know it does, because I can feel the heat of it, I can sense the tension in him, a delicious, masculine sort of vibration that makes me want to melt into him, to peel back all those proper, polite layers and discover the man beneath . . .

In the next minute, everything I thought I knew about men, everything I thought I understood about reading the moment comes to a crashing, awful halt.

Thomas leans away—not obviously, but enough to feel like a slap in the face, and clearing his throat, he stands. "This was a mistake. Me coming here, this whole complicated mess we're in—"

He runs his hand through his hair. "I apologize."

His voice is stiff, formal, as though he's talking to a stranger, and that alone makes my stomach hurt.

"Wait," I say, standing a little clumsily, my face burning red. "I'm so sorry, I misread. And Anna—"

The magnitude of my blunder crashes over me, and I want to die.

I put my hands over my face and let out a wounded groan. "I'm so sorry."

"It's not—it's—" He looks as frustrated as I feel. "It's fine, Mac. But I have to go."

And he does. He leaves, and I flop back onto the couch in a pile of humiliated regret.

Though it must be more than regret.

I must be all-out *hurt*, which makes me do insane, stupid things.

Like pick up my phone and ask the hunky trainer Kris Powers if he wants to meet up for a drink.

And then, because the night is merely okay, after one too many whiskies, I do something even stupider:

I invite Kris to join me in Vermont for a couple's bachelor–bachelorette party.

Not so much because I want him there.

But because it feels like a distraction is the only way I can survive an entire weekend of having to see Thomas with Anna.

CHAPTER FOURTEEN

Friday Morning, September 30

～

*T*homas doesn't show up at our office the next day. Or the next. And not on Friday either and I'm hit by the obvious emotion:

Relief.

But another feeling wiggles in there as well:

Disappointment?

I don't want to see him, because: Failed Kiss Horror.

And yet, I also can't escape this strange, unfamiliar sense of . . .

Missing him? As though my day without him in it isn't quite right, isn't quite full.

That can't be right. Can it?

It doesn't matter, anyway, because I don't hear from Thomas aside from a few formal work emails, and Christina was copied in on all of those. There wasn't even a hint of what he was thinking or feeling.

I don't hear from him all weekend, either. Not that I'd been expecting to.

I *do* hear from Kris, and any hope that he'll back out of the Vermont trip fades, because he actually seems kind of excited.

Though, that could be because he thinks he's finally getting in my pants.

Yeah. That's right. I didn't go home with him after that night at the bar. I'd already done one stupid thing by inviting him to Vermont, I didn't want to add another by sleeping with one man when I couldn't stop thinking about another.

I take Saturday to myself, to watch TV, do laundry, and actually, I find myself working a little, even though I'm well ahead of schedule on my deliverables and don't technically have to work.

I'm really, really loving the Fusion campaign, and all of the agency's feedback on the concepts I have sent over have been glowing.

Sunday is cool and crisp and beautiful, and I happily agree to Collette's last-minute suggestion of brunch and shopping down in SoHo. We mostly talk about the bachelor–bachelorette party, and I impress myself wildly by keeping a smile on my face the entire time, even when Thomas's name comes up.

It also makes me realize that a good friend won't let the tension with Thomas and myself get in the way of putting on an amazing weekend for Collette and Jon, so I spend the rest of Sunday with my notebook and my iPad and phone, putting together an itinerary and calling around to check on prices and availability. For all I know, I could be duplicating efforts with Thomas, but I can't quite bring myself to get in touch with him to check.

Tomorrow will be soon enough.

And then Monday rolls around, and maybe I take a tiny bit more care with my appearance. I braid my blue streak and wind it into a messy little knot all of its own, and then I curl the rest in big, loose curls that feel sort of pretty and feminine.

My outfit toes the line of what's considered "business professional" attire, but I'm feeling the need for a little armor, and I don it in the form of thigh-high boots over slim-fitting black pants and an off-the-shoulder sweater that shows my bra strap.

Which is red.

Only . . . there's no Thomas.

He's not there when I get in at eight. He doesn't show by nine. And when he's a no-show for the ten o'clock check-in call with Insurgence, I officially have a knot in my stomach.

Exactly how much damage did I do?

I'm about to find out: a lot.

At lunch time, I finally hear from Thomas via text.

Hey. Got a minute to meet me outside?

I frown. *Outside?*

Outside where?

The office.

The office? Our office?

I look out the window, and sure enough, I see him standing there. Only, he's wearing jeans. And a sweater. Not his usual work clothes, but I guess I'm not either.

Still watching him, I call him.

"Just come up here," I say when he picks up. "I brought my lunch today, and it's freezing out."

He looks up, and even though I'm several stories up, I feel it low in my gut when our eyes meet.

"Mac. Please. Come down here? You can have my coat if you need it."

There's something in his voice I don't like at all. But once again, I'm the damn moth to his flame, and a minute later I step outside, pulling on my jacket as I do so, even though it ruins the effect of my red bra strap.

"Well," I say, walking towards him and extending my hands. "I'm here. What had to happen outside instead of inside where it's warm?"

"I couldn't go inside. I don't have my key."

"Oh. Well, I'm sure Brian—"

"No." He shakes his head. "I don't have my key, because this isn't going to be my office anymore."

My stomach sinks all the way this time. "Oh, come on. What excuse did you have to come up with to explain to Christina that you can't work offsite because you're avoiding me?"

"No excuse." He shoves his hands into his pockets. "I wanted you to hear it from me first. I gave my notice on Friday afternoon. And since I was so new and there wasn't much to off-board, we all agreed that two weeks wasn't really necessary. So as of today, I'm no longer an Elodie employee."

"You—what? You *quit*? After just a couple of weeks? Doesn't that go against your creed or something?"

"It didn't feel great to bail so early in the game," he admitted. "But in my gut, I knew it wasn't a good fit. Me sticking around out of some sense of responsibility or guilt wouldn't be fair to me, the team, or my bosses."

I scowl at him. "This isn't because of last week, right? Because I *swear* that was just—"

"I quit because it was the right thing to do, Mac." There's a sharp finality to his tone and I exhale.

"Okay. Sure." I feel a little stung.

He rubs a thumbnail along his nose, looking frustrated. "So, I got your email. All that stuff for Vermont looks great. Very organized. Thanks for doing that."

"No problem!" I say, a bit too brightly. "I'm actually really looking forward to it next week. Oh! And you'll be thrilled to know you don't have to worry about my sad lonely self being all alone."

He's been distracted, but his gray-blue eyes sharpen at that, and he stares at me. "Oh yeah?"

I shrug. "V-Cut and I hung out. Had a great time, and he's down for a little New England fall getaway."

Thomas's jaw tenses. "Seriously, Mac? You're asking the guy who stood you up, who's—you barely know him, and you're bringing him to your best friend's pre-wedding celebration?"

"How is that any different from you bringing Anna to your brother's engagement party? You knew all the skeletons in her closet, did you? Oh, wait. Perfect Thomas doesn't date women with skeletons in their closets, or blue hair, or . . ."

I break off because I've just revealed way too much.

"That's great," Thomas says with a thick layer of sarcasm. "I have no doubt Kris will give you everything you've ever wanted, which is nothing."

"Thank you," I say with a sweet smile. "And congratulations on trusting your gut for the first time in your life about the job. Maybe, with enough practice, you'll even figure out how not to be the most boring person alive."

He shakes his head and turns away. "I'm sure I'll see you

around, Mac. Since the universe can't seem to get the message that we can't stand each other."

I don't stamp my foot like I want to when Thomas walks away. I do, however, cry just a little, though for the life of me I can't figure out why.

Or maybe I'm just not ready to admit it.

CHAPTER FIFTEEN

Friday Morning, October 7

⟡

*S*o, here's a fun lesson. Never, *ever* let yourself think you've hit rock bottom.

The moment you do is the second fate will let you know there is always a lower level you can be shoved to.

The Friday morning of Collette and Jon's Vermont weekend, I stare down at my phone in disbelief, reading the message over and over again, even though I know it won't change.

Babe. So sorry, can't make it this weekend. Have fun for me though!

I . . . I have no words. To put it in perspective of how very lame this is: I have my suitcase and duffle bag at my feet, and oh yeah: Kris is supposed to be my ride.

I squeeze my eyes shut, though not against tears, because unlike that awful afternoon with Thomas last week, I don't feel like crying. I'm not hurt, not really. I've hung out with Kris a couple of times in the past week just so that I didn't feel like I was taking a total stranger on the trip, but I'm not sure I even like the guy. Conversation, if you can call it that, is boring to the extreme, and even my physical attraction has cooled to an indifference. Like, Kris is still hot, but I note it in the objective kind of way, I don't feel it.

So no. Not hurt.

Pissed, though? Definitely.

Swearing up a storm as I vent to my plants (very good listeners), I text Collette to let her know what's going on and that I'll be late, even as I hate to put any sort of damper on her weekend. That's what makes me the most mad; not that he bailed on me, but that it's going to impact my best friend's bachelorette weekend.

Collette, though, as usual, is amazingly understanding, both in sharing my desire to end Kris Powers, as well as wanting to help.

Me: **Don't worry about it!! There are like five rental car places within walking distance of me, I'll figure something out.**

Collette: **Did you text Thomas? He was coordinating transport, right? Maybe he knows someone who has room for one more?**

I snort. Yeah, right. I'll just hustle to text him.

He *had* been in charge of transportation, and it had been with no small amount of satisfaction that I'd replied to his email letting him know that Kris would be borrowing his roommate's car to get there.

His comeback: **Congratulations. You're dating a grown man with a roommate.**

Yeah, okay, fine. It's a pretty solid burn. Which is exactly why I won't be contacting him to let him know that there will be no Kris, and thus no Kris's roommate's car.

Collette texts again. **Ugh, I hate this. Jon and I would have**

TOTALLY given you a ride had we not come up a day early for some couple time!

It had been Thomas's idea to arrange an extra night for the bride- and groom-to-be. An irritatingly considerate one.

Me: **Stop. Quit being nice and making me regret telling you!**

I call the closest rental car place to me and strike out. The next two basically laugh at me for trying to get a last-minute car on *a Friday*.

I'm not panicking, not quite, but Collette's next message definitely fills me with relief:

I found you a ride! Be outside in five minutes.

"Oh, thank god," I mutter, grabbing the handle of my suitcase.

I've splurged on a matching new set of luggage. My old suitcase was ancient with a janky zipper. This is one of those new, fancy suitcases with the phone charger built into it that you see Instagram influencers wheeling around looking way cuter than anyone has a right to after a twelve-hour flight.

After approximately five hundred hours of deliberation, I'd gone with the dark green option and a matching canvas duffel bag, which for the purpose of this particular trip is basically 80 percent penis paraphernalia, 20 percent toiletries. I've taken to thinking of it as my "bag of dicks." Technically, this is a co-ed party, but there's a "girls only" happy hour component of the weekend which I'm fully prepared for.

I haul my bags and the winter parka draped over my arm outside to the curb. It's only October, so the weather here in the city doesn't warrant a winter coat, but it freaking *snowed* in Vermont last week, so I've gone with sort of an après-ski theme.

I start paying attention to the cars passing by, only to realize there's no point since I have no idea who my ride is, or what car they drive. I'm sort of assuming it'll be Stephanie and Ethan Price. They're this super-adorable couple I've met a handful of times. Ethan works with Collette and Jon, and I learned at the engagement party that they live in my neighborhood.

I don't know them all that well, but if I have to spend five hours in a car with relative strangers, I'm glad it's them. Stephanie actually reminds me a little of me. On more than one occasion, we've had quite a good chat about the difficulty in finding combat boots that are both cute, and, well, combat. And I'm obsessed with her hair. The tips of her hair were a purple that definitely has me thinking that'll be my next color when I get tired of the blue streak.

A generic red car pulls up to the curb, and when the trunk pops open, I'm fairly sure that's my ride. I start wheeling my bag that way, but I skid to a halt when the driver's side door opens and *he* steps out.

"*You.*"

"Me. Again," Thomas replies, without smiling.

"*You're* my ride?" I say, unable to keep the horror out of my voice.

"Obviously, Mac," he says with a touch of impatience as he comes towards me and reaches for the handle of my bag.

His fingers brush my hand as he takes it from me, his eyes locking on me for a split-second at the contact and then jerking away as he lifts my suitcase easily into the trunk.

It says plenty about how much I love Collette that I force myself to move forward, dropping my duffel bag and parka into the trunk as I fight the tidal wave of dread at the thought of five hours with Thomas and his girlfriend.

He closes the trunk and goes back around to the driver's side without a word.

I open the back passenger side door and climb inside, slamming the door.

I stare straight ahead, which is why I see Thomas's hand—a nice hand—appear on the back of the headrest of the passenger seat as he pivots around to look at me.

"Mac. What the hell are you doing?"

I spare him the briefest of glances. "What?"

He gestures to the front seat. "Get up here."

I blink. "Isn't—"

I lurch forward, belatedly realizing that Anna's not just quiet—she's not there.

"Where's Anna?"

"Not here, obviously, and I refuse to be your chauffeur, so sit in the front seat, please."

I only hear the first part of his sentence. "She's not here, as in she's getting to Vermont a different way, or not here as in, not coming at all?"

"The latter." Thomas's expression betrays nothing, and I have a million questions, but I'm worried they'd betray too much, such as my puzzling giddiness at this news and what it might mean.

Thomas turns back around to face the front, placing both hands on the steering wheel, but makes no move to put the car in drive. He means it about me coming up to the front seat. I sigh, unclicking my seatbelt, and a moment later, I'm re-situated, and he's pulling into traffic.

"Is this your car?" I ask, glancing around at the nondescript interior. It's clean, and new-ish, but not particularly fancy.

He shakes his head. "Rental."

"Do you get out of the city often? For weekend trips?"

"No."

I sigh. "If we're going to manage to have civil conversation for the next few hours, you're going to have to give me better than one-word answers."

"Then let's not bother with conversation. I'm good with silence."

"Fine," I snap. "Can I at least turn on music?"

He gestures to the touch panel. "My phone's connected. Have at it."

After a moment of fiddling with the options, I bang my head on the headrest. "You might have mentioned you only have classical music downloaded, grandpa."

"Sorry it's not Van Halen," he says in a bored tone, as he merges onto the West Side Highway.

I look over in surprise. "You know what music I listen to?"

"We've shared a tight office space. Those headphones you wear constantly have a lot of sound leakage."

I roll my eyes, not the least bit sorry. He should be so lucky as to enjoy my music. Van Halen's "Unchained" beats the pants off Mozart.

But since it's only Mozart or silence . . .

I pick up his phone again, hitting play on the one he's labeled Favorites.

I . . . don't hate it. The flute is actually kind of soothing, maybe this ride will pass in no time at all . . .

I stare out the window, proud of how calm and zen I'm being. After a while, I turn to glance at the clock. Surely we're at least an hour in . . .

It's been seven minutes.

I sigh. Bored. I pivot a little further in my seat towards Thomas, unabashedly studying him.

"So. How's the life of leisure?" I ask. "Or have you already found another job?" I'm guessing it's that. He doesn't strike me as the type to tolerate unemployment for more than a day. I'm still shocked that he quit in the first place.

It seems so very un-Thomas.

He maintains his silence for a moment, and I worry he's going to make good on his threat to avoid conversation all the way to Vermont, but he finally relents.

"I'm going to take a few months before jumping into anything."

I fiddle with the blue streak I've wound up into a bun today as I continue to look at his profile, which is blatantly tense.

"The not jumping into something, I see. You being okay without a paycheck for a couple months? Harder to wrap my head around," I tell him.

He glances over briefly, then back at the road. "When I was nine, my dad lost his job—nothing dramatic, just a round of lay-offs, but it caught him and my mom by surprise. After that, they always made a point to maintain what they called the Ripcord Fund."

"So, like a savings account?" I ask.

"Sort of, but this was in *addition* to their regular savings. This was money specifically set aside for times when they were without work, either planned or unplanned. They instilled the importance of such a fund in my brothers and me, though I've never had cause to use it until now."

"I can't believe Elodie was that bad." *Or that working with* me *was.*

"It wasn't," Thomas says, and the way he glances over at me makes me think he heard the silent addendum. "It was more . . ." He drums his thumbs on the steering wheel, as though gathering his thoughts.

"There were a couple of reasons for me quitting," he says finally. "But one of them was that conversation you and I had the first day in the satellite office. We were talking about being a middle manager, and I heard you describing it, I heard myself describing it . . ."

"I never meant to belittle it," I say softly. "Really, I didn't."

"I know. But the conversation planted a seed of realization. I'm thirty-one. I'm not married, I don't have kids, and maybe that would chafe less if I'd been devoted to a career that I loved. But . . ."

He shrugs his shoulders.

I think on this as I turn and look out the window. "You feel stunted."

"Yes," he says, sounding surprised. "Yes, exactly. That's the perfect word."

I nod. I know it's the *perfect* word, because it sums up how I've been feeling as well. For different reasons, obviously. But neither one of us is where we expected to be by this point in our life. I'd always sort of imagined that I'd be a vagabond, maybe working in Bucharest at a stationery store, then moving on to owning a surf shop in the Caribbean, or becoming a street artist in Paris.

Instead, I have a 401k at a company whose products I can't afford myself, and even as much as I genuinely love what I'm doing, I can't shake the uncomfortable feeling that I'm *too* comfortable. It's like I feel stuck, but not because something is holding me back, but because I don't know where I'm supposed to go.

My situation isn't exactly like Thomas's, but I feel what he's feeling. It's unnerving when you wake up one day and look around to realize your life is nothing like you envisioned, yet any new, revised vision seems just out of reach and completely shrouded by impenetrable fog.

Thomas and I fall silent again, but it's less tense this time, more contemplative. Almost *companionable*, and I'm surprised that instead of grating on my nerves, the classical music becomes more enjoyable the more we listen to it. In fact, it's so relaxing I feel myself getting borderline sleepy until a sign on the highway catches my eye.

"Hey!" I press my finger to the window. "That little burger place is around here, right?"

As part of our planning process for the weekend, Thomas and I had come up with a couple of recommended food stops and scenic view recommendations to make the ask of people driving five hours a little less daunting. A cute roadside burger stand in a red barn and seasonal decor was one of the suggestions.

"You hungry?" he asks. It's barely eleven.

"A little. You?"

"I could eat."

I pick up his phone to type in the Burger Barn to his Maps app, and we let Siri work her navigational magic.

"Oh my gosh," I say as he turns into the gravel parking lot. "It's even better than it looks on Instagram!"

"Pretty sure that's the first time that statement's ever been uttered," Thomas says, pulling into an empty spot.

The barn looks exactly like what I think a barn should look like. Big and red, with just enough fading and wear-and-tear to look like the real thing rather than a prop piece. You can't actually enter the barn; the doors are the counter where you order the food, but it doesn't matter because the eating area in front is just as charming.

There are picnic tables, but instead of benches, they've got bales of hay. There are pumpkins in every color, scarecrows, and though we're past peak leaf season thanks to a cold, early autumn, the ground is covered in crunchy brown leaves that beg for boots and hot chocolate.

Basically, it's a little slice of Fall Heaven.

"I'll order, you just keep gawking," he says with a slight smile, since I already have my phone out, trying to frame up the perfect shot. "Burger?"

"Cheeseburger. Onion rings if they have them. Milkshake."

"Flavor?"

"Surprise me," I say, zooming in on an artistic corn bouquet.

When I've captured all of the cutest parts of the place, I grab my coat out of the trunk, then grab Thomas's as well. I see plenty of people eating in their car, given the cold weather, but I'm hoping he won't mind bundling up and eating at one of the tables.

I find us a table in the sun, and he joins me carrying a red tray piled high with burgers, fries, onion rings and two milkshakes.

He points at them. "Peanut butter chocolate, and birthday cake. Take your pick."

I take a cup in each hand.

"By all means, have both," he says dryly as I try one flavor, then the other.

"We'll share them," I declare. "They're too good to limit ourselves to one."

"Sure. What's a few shared germs among proclaimed enemies," Thomas replies as he lifts a cheeseburger and hands it to me.

"Exactly." Except we don't *feel* like enemies, not in this little slice of autumn wonderland, the crisp October chill softened by the warm sunshine.

The food is everything I want it to be. The burger is juicy, the fry crispy, the onion ring hot and greasy. I wash down another fry with a sip of milkshake, and let out a happy sigh.

Thomas looks pretty contented himself as he dunks a fry in ketchup, and then studies me as he chews. "You want to talk about it?"

"*It* being . . ."

"V-Cut bailing on you?" I've just bitten into an onion ring, and I freeze for a moment, before resuming chewing. Taking my time.

"Do *you* want to talk about why Anna isn't here?" I ask it rhetorically, maybe a little bit antagonistically, but he merely wipes his finger on the napkin on his knee and picks up the chocolate peanut butter milkshake. "Sure."

I try to hide my surprise. And my eagerness to know why she's not here.

"We're not seeing each other anymore," he says.

"Oh. What happened?"

Please don't be heartbroken.

The thought comes out of nowhere, and the ache it leaves in my chest is both strong and *confusing*.

"Nothing dramatic," Thomas answers. He takes another bite

of burger. "Things had been cooling off for a while. Actually . . ." He chews. "I'm not sure they ever heated up in the first place. We never really got past that first date stage. You know?"

I narrow my eyes. "What do you mean, you know? Like, I specifically know?"

"Stand down, Mac. Turn of phrase. *Interesting* reaction though," he says lightly, almost teasingly.

It *is* an interesting reaction. Not so long ago, I sort of prided myself for being "above" women who freak out about a guy not calling the next day, but for some reason, I have this bizarre desire for him to see me differently.

"Your turn to share," he says. "V-Cut."

"Ah. Kris." I reach out and take the chocolate peanut butter shake from Thomas's hand and contemplate how real to get, and decide to repay his candor with some of my own.

"Honestly?" I say. "I'm kind of relieved. Don't get me wrong, I still sort of want to kill him for leaving me in the lurch like that. But I'm not bummed that he won't be a part of this weekend."

"Even though he was exactly what you wanted?"

Was he?

I shrug in response.

"I find it rather vexing," Thomas says thoughtfully. "That Anna seemed so perfect on paper, or on the screen, as it was, and she checked all of my boxes, and yet . . ."

"Something's missing?" I supply for him.

"Right." Thomas looks frustrated. "But what?"

"Hell if I know. I mean, I only have the one box, but . . ."

"What's that?" he says, looking acutely interested.

"A V-cut, of course."

He lets out a quick, surprised laugh. "Right. Of course."

And then our eyes lock, just for a split-second, and our laughter fades as we both look away, and I wonder if we're wondering the same thing: That we may not know how to name that *something* that's missing, but we know it when we find it.

Trying to snap out of it, I give him a more thorough once over, taking in his no-hair-out-of-place cut, the great jawline that would never dare to miss a single day of shaving. The dorky cable-knit sweater, the preppy wool peacoat . . .

The only thing missing is a sign on his chest saying, "I'm not your guy, Mac."

So why then, when his fingers brush mine as he reclaims the milkshake, does my stomach explode in butterflies? Why am I *way* more curious about what Thomas has going on beneath all that buttoned-up than I was about what was beneath Kris's too-tight henleys?

"I have a proposal," Thomas says.

Yes. Yes, I accept, I will absolutely help you discover the joys of no-strings-attached sex . . .

"How about a truce for this weekend?" he continues. "For Jon and Collette's sake, we try our best to overcome our rather incredible capacity for getting beneath each other's skin."

Huh, okay, so Thomas has slightly different thoughts about skin than the ones I was having, but overall, he brings up an excellent point. I don't want to ruin Collette's weekend because I'm having funny thoughts about the best man.

"Deal," I say, extending my hand for him to shake. "From now through Sunday evening, we will be the very best of friends."

"Well, I was thinking more along the lines of just being civil, but sure," Thomas says, enveloping my hand in his and giving it a professional shake. "Friends."

Neither one of us acknowledges that we hold hands for a split-second longer than *friends*.

CHAPTER SIXTEEN

Friday, October 7

~

"*O*h my. So, so many penises, so little time."

This comes from Stephanie Price, who's perusing the bowl of penis-shaped gummies before picking up an unfortunate green, crooked one. "They don't really look like this? Do they?"

She wiggles it at me, then eats it.

"I haven't had to suffer through that, but . . ." I pick out a short, squatty red one. "This is unfortunately familiar to me."

"I can't find Ethan's in here," she says, poking through the bowl. "Guess that means I'll have to acquaint myself with the real thing very soon." She wiggles her eyebrows at me, then scans the area for her husband.

Stephanie shoots Ethan a smile that's a little bit naughty, a little bit sweet, and I can't help myself from following her line of sight. Ethan is gazing at her right back, both adoring and a little naughty himself, and I have no doubt he'll be all too happy to show his wife his non-crooked member very shortly.

We're at the afterparty, of sorts. After arriving in Vermont,

Thomas and I had settled into our respective rooms. We're on the same floor, but not adjoining.

Not that I paid close attention or anything.

Thomas may be the master planner of the weekend, and he took on all the big things: transportation, reservations, blah blah. But I took on the *important* things. As soon as I dropped off my bags, I headed back to the front desk, to ensure the party guests got their goodie bags:

Advil, bottled water, and lots of snacks. I'd thought about adding condoms in as well, but figured since everyone here is coupled up already, that sort of thing is their business.

The weekend's official kickoff had been a girls-only and boys-only happy hour at the hotel lobby bar. *Technically* we'd all been in the same space, but at separate ends of the bar for the requisite girl talk, and the guys doing their thing, which to me sounded like a lot of sports and whisky conversation.

Dinner had been Thomas's undertaking. He'd reserved a private dining room at a little farm-to-table restaurant with amazing reviews, and because he and I are friends for the weekend, I can admit the guy did good. Five stars does not do *nearly* enough justice to the spicy pumpkin sausage ravioli I'd had.

We're all back at the hotel, out on the back patio, eating leftover penis gummies in a space that's every bit as great as I was hoping it would be from the website photos. It's cold out, but everyone is bundled up, and between the enormous bonfire, the heaters, and the basket of blankets, everyone seems cozy and happy.

Most importantly, Collette and Jon seem happy. The soon-to-be bride and groom are curled up together on a huge wooden porch swing and are in full-out makeout mode now.

Actually, for that matter, *everyone* is pretty close to makeout mode. I've been so busy making sure things are going well that I haven't really had time to dwell on being the only single woman here. But all of a sudden I'm very, very aware that I'll be the only one going to bed alone tonight.

Stephanie picks up a wine bottle and tops off her glass, holding it up to me in question. I shake my head.

"So, how'd you and Ethan meet?" I ask. It's not just polite small talk; I really want to know. They're adorable together, but in an odd-couple kind of way.

She grins, reading my mind. "You mean, how did a girl in leather pants and love of black eye shadow snag Captain America?"

I smile. "Actually, I was wondering more how *he* snagged *you*."

She waggles another gummy penis at me. "I like you. I do. And as far as Ethan and I, we collided back in college, and yes, collided is the appropriate word choice. We took a film class together, got stuck as partners. Then, in a weird twist, I ended up pretending to be his girlfriend, and then in an even weirder twist, I became his actual girlfriend, and gasp, liked it. And loved him."

"Awww."

The corner of her mouth lifts in a smile as Stephanie chews her gummy. She shifts to study her husband, then tilts her head. "They look a bit alike, don't they? Ethan and Thomas?"

They look nothing alike. Ethan's hair is blond, Thomas's brown. Ethan is brawnier, Thomas more lean. Their personalities are different as well. Ethan's a charmer, all big smiles and big laughs, Thomas is . . . not that.

I think I know what she means though. They don't look alike, but they have the same . . . vibe? They're both clean cut and classically handsome. The kind of man you can imagine easily sitting at the head of a boardroom, or coaching Little League, or sipping Scotch while wearing freaking tweed.

"He watches you, you know," Stephanie says, leaning towards me slightly and lowering her voice.

I look back. "What? Who?"

"Thomas. I was sitting across from him at dinner. He looked at you whenever he thought you wouldn't notice."

My stomach flips, even as my brain rejects the idea.

I snort in skepticism.

"In fact," Stephanie adds, in a playfully taunting tone. "The only times he wasn't looking at you were when *you* were looking at *him*."

I suck in my cheeks. "I don't even like the guy."

I'm not sure who I'm trying to convince, Stephanie or myself, and her smile is sympathetic. "For the record, I didn't like Ethan either."

"Out of curiosity." She points down at the bowl of penis gummies. "Which one do you think is most like Thomas?"

"I haven't thought about it," I lie. "Though knowing him, he wouldn't tolerate anything less than absolute perfection." I pull out a perfect purple specimen.

"You'll have to let me know," she says with a wink, before waving goodbye and making her way over to her husband.

I eat the gummy—the closest I'll ever come to Thomas's member—and watch as Stephanie winds her arms around her much taller husband's waist, gazing up at him with a look that plainly says, "Take me upstairs."

Ethan is no dummy. He says something to Thomas and a few

minutes later, they're headed inside. I'm jealous. I try to tell myself it's just because of the sex part, not the romantic part, but it doesn't feel as true as it usually does. I blame the sheer cuteness of this B&B and all the couple vibes that are heating up the space more than the bonfire.

Even with the hormones and fire, it's still cold, and unlike everyone else, I don't have someone to cuddle with. I pull one of the rolled-up fleece blankets from the provided basket and make my way over to one of the swinging benches that's flanked by two heaters, and a bit closer to the fire than my current spot.

I draw my knees up to my chest and perch my phone atop them. I begin scrolling through the photos I took of Burger Barn, trying to decide which ones to edit and post to my profile.

"May I join you?" I glance up to find Thomas looking down at me, hands shoved in his pockets, and shoulders hunched a little against the cold air.

"Sure." I scoot over a little to make room, surprised when he lifts the fleece blanket and slides beneath so that we're sharing it.

His thigh presses against mine, but he doesn't seem to notice.

I definitely notice.

"We did good," he says, nodding across the fire to where Collette's head is now nestled against Jon's chest, his hand stroking over her long brown hair. "They seem happy."

"Totally. You think anyone will mind that the leaf bus tour isn't going to be very orange and red? That early snow storm that hit last week apparently shortened the foliage season this year." There. Leaves are a safe, unsexy topic, right?

"Nah. I think everyone just seems really happy to have a weekend away from the city."

I look up at his profile. "What about you? Happy to be away from the city?"

"I never mind a change of pace. You?"

"Same. Though sometimes my favorite part about leaving Manhattan is how much I love coming back to it. Suddenly the car honks and the crowded sidewalks and tiny living spaces seem charming instead of annoying when you have some distance."

"I've never thought about it that way," Thomas says thoughtfully. "But you're absolutely right."

I shrug. "It happens."

Thomas glances down, noting my upturned phone. "You can keep doing whatever you were doing."

"That's okay." I lock my phone, turning the screen black. "I can do it later."

I'd rather talk with you.

We sit in silence for a bit, both of us watching the fire, listening to it crackle. I don't mean to speak, and I really don't mean to speak about that night, but maybe it was the mention of the tiny living space, maybe it's just because I need to get it off my chest, but I hear myself say:

"I'm sorry I almost kissed you."

His head snaps my way, and I force myself to meet his eyes and keep going. "It was beyond inappropriate. You had a girlfriend, you were my boss, and most embarrassingly of all, it just . . . never would have worked."

His expression gives me nothing, and feeling more foolish than ever, I keep babbling on.

"And I just keep thinking, what if the situations were reversed, what if some dude had tried to make a move on me in all those same circumstances, and ugh, it's so cringey . . ." I finish with a laugh, but it sounds a little brittle.

Thomas turns away, facing the fire once more, the flickering light from the flames highlighting the stark, masculine planes of his features.

"Anyway. I'm *really* sorry," I say, trying to ease through the awkwardness. "Normally I'd go die now, but I figure I should wait to clean up, and—"

"I'll take care of it." His voice isn't quite curt, but it's not not a dismissal, either, and I force a smile to hide my dismay.

Obviously, that night is one that is Not To Be Mentioned, and now I've inserted a big fat wrinkle into our truce of keeping the weekend civil.

"I don't mind," he continues, his voice a little less sharp now, but not much. "Everyone looks ready to turn in anyway."

"Okay, well, if you're sure," I say with fake brightness as I start to push the blanket off my legs. "I really appreciate it."

He nods, but doesn't say anything else, and feeling awkward and embarrassed as hell, I head stiffly towards the lobby. Collette waves goodnight, and her happiness helps a little to settle me, and remind me why I'm here.

Still, I speed-walk back to my room. I may not be able to put the conversation out of my mind, but at least I can put it behind me physically. I exhale in relief once I get back to the safety of my room.

One of the reasons I chose this particular hotel over a slightly more swanky one up the road is that the rooms aren't the usual cookie-cutter hotel design and decor. Everything feels hand selected with a guest's comfort in mind. My room is entirely white, which wouldn't normally be my jam, but there's a soft, soothing vibe to the space that I need right now. A cream eyelet bedspread atop the down blanket, a bouquet of white wild flowers, even a white pumpkin on the dresser.

I'd left the window cracked just the tiniest bit, and though the room is cool, the way the sheer white drapes billow and the moonlight lights the room is so pretty that I let it be.

My conversation with Thomas is still swirling in my mind, and my gaze goes to the white clawfoot tub and the complimentary bath bubbles. I can't outrun my conversation with Thomas, but maybe I can wash it away?

I turn on the faucet and add a generous amount of apple-scented bubbles. As the tub fills, I pull my hair into a messy bun, then carefully pull out the blue streak, letting it frame my face. I don't know why, but I need that little piece of myself, that reminder of who I am.

I sink into the tub, and it's everything I want it to be. The heat feels extra gratifying given the coldness of the room, the slight breeze keeps the steam from being stifling, and the bubbles come to the point of nearly overflowing, but not quite.

The only thing missing is music, and I contemplate getting my phone, but decide against it when I realize the music I want to listen to is classical, which makes me think of him.

I stay in the tub until the cooling water starts to take a turn towards uncomfortable. There's an apple-scented lotion to match the bubbles, which I slather on liberally before wrapping myself in a white towel.

I feel better, I do, but irritatingly, I'm not quite tired yet. Or maybe I just know that when I close my eyes, Thomas's stern, unsmiling face will be all I see.

Maybe I'll read.

Real talk, I'm one of those people who always *wants* to be a reader, but I never quite seem to make time for it until right before bed, which basically means . . . reading puts me to sleep more often than not.

And since I'm hoping sleep will dull the edges of my lingering humiliation, I grab my phone and crawl onto the bed, sitting cross-legged as I scroll through purchased ebooks.

The knock is quiet.

So quiet that I think it's my imagination at first, but then it comes again, a little louder.

I wrinkle my nose in confusion. *Collette?*

I look through the peephole and my lips part in surprise. Not Collette. Not even close.

I open the door before thinking it through, and Thomas is clearly taken aback at the sight of me in nothing but a hotel bathrobe.

"What's up?" I say, crossing one bare foot atop the other to try and contain my nervousness. "Everything okay downstairs? Broken wine glass—oh crap, I forgot my penis gummies!"

He smiles a little at that. "I believe Erika and Ben took the bowl to their room, for reasons I don't want to know."

"Ah. So . . .?"

He swallows and glances down. Then back at me. "I didn't want it to happen like that."

"The conversation about the kiss?" I say, resting my hand on the door jamb, my head on the hand. "Yeah. I clunked it up, I'm sorry. I was trying to ease my conscience and instead made everything awkward."

"Not the conversation."

I shake my head. *I don't understand.*

He runs his hand through his hair, then frowns at me. "You drive me fucking nuts, Mac."

I let out a little laugh, surprisingly not the least bit surprised, because . . . "You drive me nuts too. But I thought for the weekend . . ."

"I don't mean you annoy me, though you do. I don't mean that you're not aggravating and stubborn, because you are. I mean you drive me fucking nuts in that I can't stop—I've never . . ."

He reaches out and lifts my blue streak of hair, studying it for a moment, then winding it around his finger gently, his gaze tracking the movement of his finger.

"I didn't want to kiss you when I was with Anna. I didn't want to kiss you when I was your boss."

"That makes sense," I say, my voice all low and raspy and hard to hear over the pounding of my heart.

His silver eyes come back to mine, but they're not cool now, they're stormy and gray. "I didn't want it to go like that," he says, repeating his earlier statement.

Thomas eases closer to me, releasing my hair and instead sliding an arm around me, his hand on my back. "Because I wanted it to go like this."

His palm flattens over the small of my back, firm and possessive as he presses me to him. Then he dips his head, and his mouth closes over mine.

CHAPTER SEVENTEEN

Friday, October 7

*O*h god.

Oh *god*.

He's a good kisser. The realization is as jarring as it is welcome, because any hope I'd held that we just needed to get this out of our system, to verify what our first impressions already knew— *not a match*—goes out the window.

We may not be soulmates, we may not even fully like each other, but . . . we fit.

The way his mouth moves over mine, the way I respond to him—it erases any kiss I've had in the past year—the past decade.

He was supposed to be timid! my brain protests feebly.

Timid, Thomas Decker is not. His mouth is firm and sure, expertly teasing mine in searching, pulling kisses, a silent, persistent demand to open to him, to concede.

I do on a soft sigh, as his tongue coaxes mine into a deeper kiss.

My hands lift to his chest, his shoulders, until my arms are linked all the way around his neck, pulling him closer.

My breasts are pressed against his chest, soft to his hard, and I'm short to his tall. *We fit.* We fit really, really well, and I know he notices too, because he growls low in his throat, a palm moving over my ass, cupping, squeezing, claiming, without apology.

I kiss him back with all the pent-up frustration of the past weeks, my fingers messing that too-tidy hair, my body aching with the pressing, relentless need for more.

It's the urgency of it, the sheer craving that terrifies me, and has me pulling my mouth from his, breathing hard.

His eyes search mine, both hot and frustrated.

"If we do this," I say on a pant, "we do this my way. I don't want flowers, I don't want to meet your mother, and I won't be your little woman."

His fingers close around both of my wrists, lifting my arms above my head as he pushes me backwards, pressing me to the door, my hands pinned above my head.

His mouth easily finds my neck where the robe has loosened from our wiggling, his breath is hot against my neck, his words low and raspy. "I didn't bring flowers," he says, his tongue flicking over my skin. "I sure as hell am not thinking about my mother right now. But—"

His teeth scrape lightly my throat. "I am going to make you my woman. Just for tonight."

It's not a question, but I answer him anyway, my hands digging into his hair, hauling his mouth back to mine. *Yes. Yes. Yours.*

And he's mine. For now, just for now, he's mine. Knowing we're on the same page emboldens me, and my hands move more confidently over him, exploring everything I can reach—the corded muscles of his back, his flat torso, the hard planes of his chest.

His mouth is greedy on mine, as though he's been starving for this. For me. My fingers slip beneath his sweater, finding hot, male skin and he hisses out a breath and pulls back.

"Be sure, Mac. Be very sure."

In response, I lick the center of my bottom lip.

"Alright," he says gruffly. "Alright."

His hands have been exploring me over the robe, almost chaste in comparison to the boldness of his mouth, but now they move over me with purposeful teasing, fingers digging into my hips, palms brushing over the sides of my breasts, idly, deliberately . . .

I moan a little in frustration, and he captures my lip between his teeth, nipping at the exact moment his hands cover my breasts.

"That," he murmurs, his palms opening wide, teasing the tips through the robe. "That what you need?"

I swallow and manage to shake my head.

"No?" His hand slips into the V of the robe, but barely, the backs of his fingers hot against my collarbone. "This?"

Again, a shake of my head, resisting the urge to arch into him, fighting to maintain control.

"Hmm." He frowns, as though baffled. Holding my gaze, his hand drifts downwards, his knuckles pressing ever so slightly into the top swell of my breast.

"Closer," I manage.

He continues to stroke there, agonizingly, the motion of his hand slowly opening the robe, bit by bit as though by accident, until it's loosened enough for his hand to slide down a bit farther.

I let out a loud moan as his fingers make fleeting contact with my aching nipple.

"Ah," Thomas says in satisfaction. "Here."

He loses all pretend hesitancy now, his fingers teasing the tip of my breast, rolling it, flicking it, pinching it, slowly notching up my pleasure until I think I might die from it.

I feel his other hand at the belt of my robe, slowly tugging it free until my robe falls open, the rush of cool air against my heated skin making me gasp.

Then I gasp for another reason as his tongue flicks over my nipple, just once, a hot, wet brush with heaven.

He scatters kisses over my chest, the sides of my breasts, the undersides, leaving the aching tip wanting.

My head moves restlessly against the door. "Thomas."

"Mac," he says, his eyes flicking up to mine, and the sight of him so close, but not where I need . . .

I take his cheeks in my hand and push his head down, and he answers the silent request immediately, lips closing over the tip of my breast, tongue rolling around my nipple in soft, hot licks.

He takes his time, giving my other breast equal treatment. I've always imagined that being with nice guys must be boring, tepid, routine, but I realize now there's an advantage to sex with a gentleman I hadn't considered—Thomas is patient, generous, gently pushing away my hands when I try to hurry things along, to give some sort of pleasure in return.

By the time his palm strokes over my belly, his hand slipping between my legs, I think I might die from the agony of being held on the brink of pleasure without release.

Even now, he takes his time, fingers stroking the folds of my sex without parting them, touching, but not delivering.

I let out a choked, furious laugh. "I hate you."

He presses just a bit harder, parting the folds a bit more, teasing the wetness even as he withholds relief.

"I mean it. I'm going to make you pay," I say, my hips tilting towards his hand.

I see him grin seconds before he kisses me, and as his tongue finds mine, his finger finds me, stroking me deftly, exploring me. I gasp into his mouth as his finger rubs my clit in ever-tightening circles. A long finger eases inside me and I break the kiss, gasping for air now, realizing that his slow and steady foreplay has me on the edge of a massive orgasm.

His silver eyes hold my eyes and he nods once. *Come.*

As if I could stop it.

My body is so tightly wound, my need built so high that when my body releases, I feel as though I may come apart. I use my hand to stifle my cries, but honestly I'm not sure how successful I am. I'm not sure of anything other than the fact that I have never come this hard, never felt this good, and we haven't even gotten to the main event.

As I try to catch my breath, Thomas eases my hand away from my mouth, kissing me with kisses that are perhaps meant to soothe, but incredibly, impossibly seem to light my need all over again.

Enough. Enough of this. My turn.

I use my hands to push at his shoulders, getting just enough leverage to scoot out between him and the door, using the element of surprise to reverse our positions, maneuvering his back to the door.

I rub against him and bite my lip before stepping back slightly. I roll my shoulders back. Shrug.

The robe falls, and Thomas swallows as I stand naked before him, his eyes hungry as they travel over me.

His way worked well—really well. Slow and steady and patient is his way.

But my way—fast, immediate, and bold—I've learned that works as well.

I hold his gaze as I drop to my knees, my fingers deftly unbuckling his belt and unfastening his jeans as he manages my name on a hoarse cry.

His boxer briefs are black. Designer logo. In my way.

I ease them down and without preamble take him in my mouth.

"Jesus fucking christ," I hear him mutter. I'd smile if my mouth wasn't full. My way works just fine.

His fingers tunnel into my mussed hair, gripping hard. His hips tilt forward and I murmur in approval. Thomas takes my cue and slowly, methodically rocks his hips forward, using my mouth for his own pleasure.

A pleasure I want him to finish, here, like this, both to return the favor, and because making Thomas Decker come undone is just about the hottest thing I've ever experienced. Hearing his groans, the quickening of his breath, and the tightening of his fingers in my hair . . .

Abruptly, he pulls me away, his hands hooking beneath my arms, hauling me up for a hard kiss before he kicks off his shoes and pants, then shoves me backwards, none too gently.

Our gazes lock and clash as I walk backwards towards the bed, him following, me, prey, him, hunter.

The back of my legs hit the bed, and I crawl back onto it. He removes his sweater and undershirt then follows me, climbing over me, making me feel small and feminine and very, very horny.

I see a glint of foil and blink in surprise. "Where'd that come from?"

"Pant pockets," he says, tearing the condom wrapper open with his teeth, and then rolling it on.

I smile. "I should have known you were a Boy Scout."

"Damn straight," he says, his hands sliding up my shins, palms cupping my knees, lifting them, spreading my legs for him.

His hand eases between my thighs, fingers slicking through the moisture, testing my readiness.

"Yes," I whisper when he glides a finger inside me easily. "This."

"That?" he says. "Or this?" He adds another finger and then hooks them both upwards.

"Oh my god," I arch. "Thomas."

"Why?" he mutters, almost to himself. "Why do I like hearing you say my name so goddamn much?"

He withdraws his hands and settles over me. I feel the tip of his cock glide through my folds, seeking, searching—

His hips push forward, and he glides inside me slowly, easily, perfectly.

"Fuck," I hear him groan, once he's all the way inside me, or maybe it was me? And then it's both of us, cursing, grasping, arching as he moves inside of me, my legs around his waist, his hands beneath my waist.

"It wasn't supposed to be this good," I pant in his ear, as his arm hooks beneath my leg, opening me wider.

"I know," he rasps. "I know."

For some reason, it's that—that acknowledgement that I'm not alone in this earth-shattering, life-altering desire that sends me over the edge of a second orgasm.

This time it's his mouth instead of my hand that captures my cries, and feeling his body tense, feeling his own relief coincide with mine is almost better than the orgasm itself.

Long moments—minutes—hours?—later, Thomas eases out of me and rolls onto his side, his arm coming up to cover his eyes as he gasps for air.

I roll towards him, propping up on one elbow. "Shoot. We are really bad at this *friends* thing."

He lets out a hoarse laugh. "Yeah. Yeah we are."

Then his arm comes up, looping behind me, easing me down to his chest. I know I should resist, I do. This breaks all the rules—*my* rules.

And yet his chest against my cheek feels so good, the heat of his body against mine feels impossible to resist.

"Why's it so cold in here?" he murmurs.

"I like to sleep with it cold. Don't you?"

"Certainly not."

"One more reason," I say, a little drowsily, "why this can only be a one-time thing. We can't even agree on temperature."

"Agreed," Thomas says softly.

I'm not sure who we're trying to convince. The other person— or ourselves.

CHAPTER EIGHTEEN

Saturday, October 8

⌒

It's still dark when I wake up the first time, protesting a little at being jostled as an arm slides beneath me. My protest is even louder at the lack of warmth I'd been cuddled against, but subsides as blankets are resettled over me. I think maybe a hand touches my hair, but I'm not sure.

When I wake up the second time, it's to an alarm, and the sun's coming in the window.

I wrinkle my nose in confusion, my groggy brain trying to sort out a few things:

1. Why I don't remember setting my alarm.
2. Why it's on the pillow next to mine instead of the nightstand.
3. Why it's playing some classical crap instead of Van Halen's "Jump."

Then all of the pieces come together.

Thomas set my alarm. Thomas set it on the pillow he vacated. Thomas changed it to his music.

I smile. I shouldn't, but I do.

By the time I shower, dress, and put on makeup, my smile is somewhat more forced as I try to fight through the possible awkwardness that awaits me at breakfast.

Maybe I'll get lucky though. The hotel has an included breakfast from six to ten am, and there's no guarantee he and I will show up at the same time. And the first planned event—wine-tasting—isn't until eleven.

And yeah, we're going to be drinking wine at eleven—what of it?

Luck is on my side. Thomas isn't at one of the buffet lines or one of the lobby tables, but Collette is, and she waves me over enthusiastically after I grab a bagel and cream cheese, plus a banana.

"Morning!" she beams. "How'd you sleep? The beds are fabulous, right?"

"Totally," I agree, taking a sip of coffee to hide the fact that the fabulous part of my bed wasn't the sleep so much as what came before—literally.

"Hey, Jon," I say to Thomas's brother, whose head is buried in the sports page.

"Morning, Mac." He grins at me over the paper, then resumes reading.

I set about spreading cream cheese on my bagel—I like lots, so I grabbed two of the little tubs, and look up only when I find Collette watching me with narrowed eyes.

"What?" I ask, freezing mid-bite.

"Jon," she says mildly. "Go away."

He looks up in surprise. "I'm sorry?"

"Go. Away."

Her fiancé opens his mouth as though to protest, then shrugs, folds his paper, and takes it and his coffee cup to another table with his cousin and his wife.

"You got *sex*," Collette says, lowering her voice so only I can hear.

"What?" My voice is bad-actress levels of scandalized. "Don't be crazy."

"Oh, shut up. I'm your best friend, and we used to live together. I know your post-coital face." She narrows her eyes. "Oh my god. Not just sex. You got *fancy* sex."

"What the heck is fancy sex? Actually, no, don't tell me. I don't want to know."

"Fancy sex," she continues anyway, "is sex that's so good, so epic, that it's above all other sex."

"I assure you, I've never had fancy sex. Just regular sex. And not recently," I rush to add. *So many lies in one little sentence.*

"You're lying." She drums her manicured nails on the table, studying me. "But why? Why would you be lying to your best friend about good sex unless . . ."

Her lips part as she puts the pieces together. "Wait a second. There is only one person here you could have had sex with."

"How do you figure that math? There are plenty of men here."

"But only one single man," she says smugly.

"In our party, sure. Maybe I slept with the bartender."

"He did *look* like your type with all those tattoos and the tongue stud," Collette admits. "Except when he was pouring my sauvignon blanc, he and I got to chatting about wedding details. He's getting married on Valentine's Day. To a Michael."

"Fascinating stuff," I say, wiping a bit of cream cheese from the corner of my mouth.

"Okay, stop playing it cool! You slept with Thomas!" she says excitedly. "Oh my God, Mac, we're going to be sisters?!"

I choke on my bagel. "Okay. Okay, calm down." I glance around, to make sure Thomas hasn't entered the room. "We did sleep together. *But*," I add before she can squeal. "It was a one-time thing. He's not going to become my boyfriend, much less my husband."

"But—"

"No," I say, lifting my hand and making a shush motion. "I love you, I'd do anything for you, but not give my life away to a guy. Especially not that guy."

She sighs. "You're still anti-matrimony? Even seeing how happy Jon and I are?"

"I'm not anti-matrimony," I correct her gently. "I'm anti-matrimony *for me*. There's a big difference."

"Huh." She lifts the string of her tea bag and bounces it in her mug as she watches me. "So you guys are just . . . boink buddies?"

"One-time boink buddies. Scratching an itch. Now that it's scratched, we'll go back to being just friends for the remainder of the weekend, and then civil acquaintances in the future."

Collette is smiling, more to herself than at me, and I narrow my eyes. "Why are you smirking?"

"Nothing," she says, all sweet innocence. "Just really looking forward to watching this day unfold."

~

Determined to prove Collette wrong, I make sure to talk to Thomas at the first possible moment so awkwardness doesn't have a chance to form.

The hotel has a free shuttle to the wineries, and I can tell he's surprised when I plop down beside him.

"You weren't at breakfast," I say.

"I was, just late. I wanted to get in a run first."

I stare at him, aghast. "A run. You are the *worst*."

"If it makes you feel better, it wasn't my best run. For some reason, I had a little less energy than usual."

"Hmm." I suck in my cheeks. "I'm so sorry to hear that."

"Yes. You sound devastated," he says, a smile in his voice.

"Collette knows about last night," I whisper, scrunching down a little in the seat and lowering my voice.

He doesn't look as surprised or dismayed as I expected. Instead, he shrugs. "Jon knows as well. He saw me on my way out to my run, and without me saying a word, he just grinned his shitty face off."

I laugh at the description. "Collette says she thinks I had Fancy Sex."

He looks down at me, interested. "Did you?"

I peer up at him. "No."

His gray gaze narrows, and I grin. "Maybe?"

I nearly add a sassy retort about needing a repeat to know for sure, until I remember that we're not doing repeats, that a do-over would make things . . . complicated.

"Can I see your phone?" I ask, extending a palm.

"Um, no."

"Please? Just for a sec. I want to look something up."

He shakes his head. "No, you want to change my alarm song to something terrible to get back at me."

My laugh is startled. "Wow. Maybe you know me better than I thought. Quick, what's my favorite color?"

Thomas glances at my hair. "Blue?"

I touch the colored part of my hair, though today I've interspersed the blue with the blonde in a French braid, rather than style it in its own way.

"Yes. But, I like to think the fact that my hair is colored in something other than blonde or brown that makes the statement, not the color itself."

"And what statement is it making?"

I consider his question seriously, because I guess I've never had to answer it aloud before. "I suppose, it says that I may have the office job, and have lived in the same building for years, but that I'm still me."

"And who are you?"

I scowl at him. "You ask annoying questions."

"Annoying, because you don't know how to answer?" he challenges.

"I know who I am," I shoot back.

But as I say it, I wonder if it's true. Because even when talking to Thomas drives me crazy, I find I never want our conversations to end.

And that doesn't sound like me at all.

CHAPTER NINETEEN

Saturday, October 8

The wine at the tasting is mediocre, at best, but nobody seems to mind, and by the time we get to lunch at an artisanal pizza place, everybody is in jovial moods. Everyone easily seems to find their spot around the long wooden table, and I'm not sure if I find him, or he finds me, but somehow Thomas and I are seated beside each other, just as we'd been on the bus, and again at the winery.

Math, I tell myself. It's simple math, that we are the only non-couple, and us pairing up makes sense.

For logistical reasons. Of course.

Collette's and Stephanie's smirks say exactly what they think of my logic, so I ignore them.

The restaurant is an excellent pick by Thomas. Lots of windows, an open-concept kitchen with a huge pizza oven. It's the kind of place that puts artisanal honey on their specialty pizzas and serves cocktails in mason jars.

"Now, see," I mutter to myself, as I peruse the menu. "This is why people have boyfriends."

"Why's that?" Thomas asks.

"Because I can't decide between the chicken and waffles pizza with Vermont maple syrup, or the meatball sub pizza. But if I had a boyfriend, I could force him to order one, and then I could eat half of each and die happy."

After a moment, he sets down his menu. "I'll be your boyfriend. For the purpose of this meal."

I give him a narrow-eyed look, and he gazes levelly back. "Relax, Mac. I offered to split pizza with you. I'm not trying to bring you home for Thanksgiving dinner."

The very thought of *that* is laughable.

"Okay then," I say, stacking my menu atop his. "I accept your pizza-splitting offer. For the duration of this meal, we are effectively going steady. Which means I get a sip of your drink." I reach over and pick up his cocktail, which looks delicious.

It's good. Tequila and something a little spicy. But it's not as good as my blueberry-lemon vodka cocktail, which he helps himself to with a grimace.

Looking around at the table, everyone by their significant others, heads bent over menus, debating options, I'm forced to admit that Thomas had been maybe a little right when he'd warned Collette and Jon that me being the lone single person might . . . suck.

I would have made the best of it; it's not like it's my first time being the only one flying solo amidst a flock of love birds. But if Thomas had been here with Anna? My stomach knots up just thinking about it.

Yikes.

I need to ground myself here. He and Anna may not have worked out, but some day, he's going to meet another Anna, another girl who's not Van Halen-loving with blue hair, someone who would never wear bikini bottoms to work because she forgot to do laundry.

Wanting to remind myself of our differences, I turn towards him. "So that I can know what ghosts of your past I'm up against in our newfound relationship. What's your longest relationship?"

He turns towards me as well, an elbow on the back of his chair. "Ever?"

"Ever."

He thinks about this. "Not counting my intense crush on Lara Croft as a kid?"

I shake my head. "Has to be a real person."

Thomas doesn't hesitate. "That would be Janie."

My easy smile slips and I feel blood leave my cheeks. How had I forgotten?

"Ah," he says lightly. "I see from that *oh shit* expression, you've heard about her."

"Jon mentioned her," I say, since I'm a terrible liar and have no poker face.

Thomas shoots his oblivious brother an irritated glare across the table. "Did he?"

I nod. "He said you were almost engaged."

"'Almost' would be the key word there. I never proposed."

"But you were planning on it?"

Thomas spins his cocktail glass with a frown. "Yeah. Yeah, I was."

Our conversation derails as the server comes around to take orders, but even after I've ordered my chicken and waffles pizza—Thomas got the meatball sub—I'm still wrapped up in my thoughts about Thomas and a woman I've never met.

"Just do it," he says in resignation.

"What?"

"Ask whatever you're thinking about Janie."

The server places a couple of focaccia on the table and Thomas reaches for it, placing a piece on my bread plate before his own, as though it's the most natural thing in the world. He's good at this boyfriend thing.

"Are you sure?" I ask, nibbling at a piece of the bread.

He nods.

"Okay, well. I guess I'm wondering, how, after going through something like that, you still want to do it again some day. If it were me, that would be the ultimate proof that people *aren't* supposed to find just the one person, and settle down forever."

Thomas doesn't get defensive. Instead he seems to think my question over as he dunks a piece of bread in the oil, chews thoughtfully, before answering. "Did Jon mention that Janie left me because she got back together with her ex?"

I nod.

"Okay, so. They're still together. Married, living in London. Twin girls, and a boy on the way, at least as of her last Christmas card. Viewed differently, isn't that proof that two people can be happy together? It's just that I wasn't meant to be the other half in that particular scenario."

"You get Christmas cards from your ex?" I ask, appalled.

He shrugs. "We're friendly."

"Huh. When we break up, you'll be getting no Christmas card from me."

"Not a problem. Knowing our luck, we'll continue to run into each other over and over until the end of time," Thomas says, smiling.

"Too true," I say. "I have no doubt that someday I'll have my sketchbook in Central Park and I'll see you walk by pushing some high-tech stroller with your shiny-haired wife—no blue in *her* hair—beside you wearing some sort of chic dress. You guys are probably coming from some museum where you have annual passes that you actually use."

"Quite possibly," he replies affably. "But that's then. For right now, I'm quite content to be in Vermont with my *current* girl-friend and her blue hair."

I prop my chin on my hand and grin at him. "I bet she's pretty great."

"I'll confess to being surprised, sometimes, how much I like her."

"Is that so," I say lightly, hating how much I want it to be true. "I'll bet she's *really* good in bed. Gives excellent head."

Thomas's low groan as he shifts in his chair is the best thing I've heard since, well . . . his groans last night.

The rest of the day is pretty perfect, and though Thomas's and my "relationship" was supposed to last only long enough to enjoy two varieties of pizza (both delish, by the way, with the chicken and waffle winning by a hair), the couple-y vibe continues after that as well.

At the distillery, where we'd found ourselves touring the

grounds together after the group tasting. On the shuttle, where we always sat beside each other, our knees brushing against each other's just a little too comfortably.

Then *again*, at dinner, where the elegant atmosphere had been more suited to quiet chatter than loud, big-group conversation, Thomas and I found ourselves talking about all those nothings that somehow feel like *something*.

And now, at the end of the night, our group finds itself in a repeat of last night, minus penis gummies, ending the evening bundled up around the bonfire.

I can't remember if I sat on the swinging bench first or if Thomas did, but somehow we end up together sharing a blanket as the group plays an enthusiastic game of *I've Never*.

And when the game ends, and the group disperses, some to bed, others to their quiet conversations, neither Thomas or I move.

I tell myself it's because I'm comfy and cozy, and I am. But I'm also . . . content. More so than I can ever remember being, and the realization leaves me feeling, ironically, a bit unsettled.

It's just one day, I remind myself. It won't kill you. One weekend.

On Monday, we'll go back to not seeing each other, at least until that future day when I probably will see him and his perfect wife and baby.

A couple of weeks ago, the thought would have made me feel a little smug. Better him than me.

Now, it just leaves me feeling melancholy, so I shove it away and remind myself what my mother told me far more often than she ever told me to eat my vegetables:

To live in the moment. This moment, right here—that was life. And life, right now, is good.

When my sleepiness increases, and my cheek finds its way to his shoulder, I feel his chin brush over the top of my head. Rest there.

I apparently fall asleep at some point, because when Thomas gently nudges me awake, everyone else is gone, and the hotel staff is extinguishing the bonfire for the night.

"Sorry," I say, feeling a bit awkward, as I wipe my mouth, checking for drool. For good measure, I wipe his shoulder too.

"No problem," he says.

We're silent as we make our way up to my room, not saying a word until we stop outside my door.

I fish my key out of the back of my jean pockets. "Well." My voice is hushed. "Thanks for being a great temporary boyfriend."

"Not as terrible as you thought?"

"No," I admit. "But don't go getting any crazy ideas about a permanent arrangement."

My voice is joking, but Thomas doesn't smile back as he steps a bit nearer. "You do that constantly, Mac. Make comments about the temporary nature, how you're not that kind of girl. Who are you trying to remind? Me? Or yourself?"

"You," I retort quickly, before thorny, life-twisting thoughts can sneak in. "It's just . . . the thing is." I huff. "I actually am kind of starting to think you're a good guy, and I don't want to hurt you."

He is silent for a minute, then nods. "I see. That irresistible, are you? That I won't be able to help myself? Fall wildly in love? Buy us a house in Connecticut?"

I flinch. "When you put it that way, it makes me sound—"

"Incredibly full of yourself? As though perhaps you underesti-
mate me? Think I'm not capable of making up my own mind, of
knowing my own heart? That I'm little more than a marriage-
seeking robot rather than a man who sometimes has just good
old-fashioned male needs?"

He's right. He's so right, it's embarrassing. Not once has
Thomas ever even remotely implied he sees me as a part of his
future. Just like he's not a part of mine.

He is, however, right here, right now, and every part of me is
aching for a repeat of last night.

I toy with the end of my braid and look up at him. "Male needs,
you say?"

Thomas nods, steps closer, lifting a hand to my face, cupping
my cheek. "Think you might be able to help me with those?"

His head lowers, his lips brushing over mine, a kiss meant to
both wait for my answer and sway it his way. But I don't need any
swaying. My arms lift, find their way around his neck like it's the
most natural thing in the world.

It's a lovely sort of kiss, both slow and sweet, and yet a little bit
extra hot knowing we're in a hushed hallway, where anyone could
come upon us making out.

His hands glide over me, and when his palms brush the sides
of my breasts, I make a needy noise that's just a little too loud and
we both freeze.

With a sheepish smile, I hold up my room key. "We could
make the one-night thing a two-night thing."

"Twist my arm," he says without hesitation. Though before I
can open the door, he grabs my hand and tugs me down the hall.
"Not your refrigerator room. Mine."

His room is cozy and warm, and we're reaching for each other in the darkness even before the door clicks quietly closed.

It's the last night in Vermont, the last night of this, and we both know it. Our kisses are slow and unhurried, our pace intentionally controlled as our hands reacquaint themselves with the other's body.

It shouldn't be like this, I think in frustration as he shoves my coat off my shoulder, his hands gliding under my sweater, his fingers cool against my skin.

My reaction to him last night, the sheer epicness of it, it should have been a result of the newness, a simple build-up of our strange chemistry.

With curiosity abated, I shouldn't want him this much, I shouldn't feel as though I'll die if he doesn't touch me, or that I'm at my most alive when he does.

He pulls my sweater over my head, then bends, pressing hot kisses to the place where my breasts swell above my bra. Thomas pulls back slightly, running a long finger along the top of the black lace.

I feel a little stab of relief that it's one of my best bras, one that I'd packed when I thought I'd be sharing a room with Kris . . .

The thought is jarring. Uncomfortable, as though trying on shoes that don't fit, and then I see the deep line between Thomas's eyebrows, realize he's had the same thought.

"Hey." I lay my palm along his jaw. "I'm glad I'm here with you."

I put an ever-so-slight emphasis on you, but when his troubled expression doesn't change, I step closer, placing my hands on his chest and going to my toes. I kiss him. I tell him with my kiss what my words can't explain, and I feel the moment he gets it. His mouth softens beneath mine, his tongue gliding inside my mouth to take command of the kiss, as his fingers unsnap the button of my jeans.

I gasp when he surprises me by sliding a hand down my front, slipping beneath lace, finding me already wet and aching.

"Believe me now?" I say on a pant, as he circles and strokes.

Thomas eases back, then drops to his knees, removing my boots and then peeling my jeans down my legs, tossing them aside.

His thumb glides over the lace V of my underwear, then he presses a hot kiss to that same spot, using his tongue to press the rough lace against my core and I cry out, my hands fisting in his hair.

I bite back my disappointment when he stands again, let him nudge me back to the bed. I sit, but before I can scoot back towards the headboard, his fingers wrap around my hips, holding me still.

His silver eyes lock onto mine as his fingers hook beneath the elastic, and I lift my hips slightly so he can ease them down, over my legs. Once more, he drops down in front of me, his hands parting my legs wide.

He kisses the inside of my knee. The other. His lips drift over the insides of my thighs, idly, as though there's all the time in the world and I'm not aching for him.

"Thomas," I groan, when he gets torturously close, then drifts back towards my knee.

"Hmm."

"Don't hmm me," I say with a laugh of frustration.

He looks up, his smile wicked. "You want something?"

It's the same game as last night. One I'm surprised by how much I like, putting words to my needs—my wants.

"Kiss me," I manage on a whisper.

He pecks the inside of my knee.

"No," I groan, my fingers tunneling into his hair. "*Lick* me."

His tongue flicks, again over the inside of my knee.

Evil, evil man.

I tug harder, guiding his head, positioning his face at the apex of my thighs.

I nearly come off the bed at the first teasing flick of his tongue, and he sets a hand low on my belly, holding me still as he licks me a second time, this time with the flat of his tongue, licking all of me, doing something devilish to my lip that has me letting out a sob and falling back onto the bed. I release his hair, instead gripping my own in a futile attempt to stay in control.

I'm never in control, not around this man, not with his head between my legs, licking me over and over with an infuriating variation in speeds, bringing me close and then making me wait.

"I need to come," I finally gasp. "Please."

A finger slips inside me as his mouth closes over my clit, circling in perfect, relentless rhythm. He adds a second finger, and I shatter, convulsing over and over with an orgasm that robs me of all thought and reason.

I'm so lost in the aftershocks that I barely register him moving away, or the sound of a condom wrapper.

But then he moves on top of me, gliding into me with a hard, perfect stroke, making me gasp his name. Hearing him groan mine.

If you would have asked me my thoughts on missionary before this weekend, I'd have said meh. But there's nothing meh about Thomas's body covering mine, his cock moving inside me, setting the pace.

His elbows are on either side of my head, his fingers in my hair. His silver eyes watching my face as he fucks me fast and hard, then slow and teasing.

He watches me as he slides a hand between our bodies, rubbing in exactly the right spot to make me come again. Only when he thrusts inside me one last time, throwing his head back as he comes with a harsh groan, does he release my gaze.

I close my own eyes in relief, at being relieved of my confused feelings, but then he lowers to me once more, his weight heavy and warm and welcome, and I realize I'm wrong.

There's no relief from the want. And I'm more confused than ever.

CHAPTER TWENTY

Sunday, October 9

~

"*Y*ou're the best. The best, the best, the very bestest . . ." Collette punctuates each "best" with a smacking kiss on my cheek, and I laughingly push her away.

"Easy, you're practically a married woman. And you're welcome, but it was nothing. Thomas did most of the hard stuff."

She releases me, tucking her hair behind her ears. "That's not what he told Jon."

I narrow my eyes.

"Oh, don't give me that trademark cynical Mac look. You're allowed to be complimented."

"He's not my boss anymore," I grouse. "I don't need his positive reinforcement."

She crosses her arms and tilts her head, giving me a speculative, best-friend study. "He *really* gets to you, doesn't he?"

"What? No." But even as I say it, I give a quick glance around the parking lot, where everybody is packing up their cars and hugging out their goodbyes. Thomas is over by Jon, laughing at something his brother said.

He doesn't laugh very often, but I like when he does.

"Oh my," Collette murmurs.

"What?" I look back at her.

"Nothing!" She smiles too brightly. "Regardless of whether or not you want to take credit, this weekend was seriously great. Jon and I were just saying this morning how we could not have imagined a better send-off into married life."

I laugh. "You like it because it practically *was* married life. There were no strippers, no debauchery . . ."

She gives a happy sigh as she looks towards her soon-to-be-husband. "Two weeks, Mac. I don't think I've ever looked forward to something as much as becoming that man's wife."

If you say so.

But since it isn't the time for, as she puts it, my Mac cynicism, I give her a tight squeeze, and make my way over to Thomas's car to wait for him.

I'm startled by a quick hug from behind, and turn to see Stephanie Price grinning at me.

"Hey!"

"Okay, I know we already said our goodbyes, and I have your phone number and I will be texting you for a hang soon," she says, giving a quick glance over her shoulder and lowering her voice. "But really quick . . ."

She looks back at me, and her face turns a little bit serious, but no less kind. "I'm going to offer some unwanted advice, and you can't say no, because it's for your own good."

I look down at my faux-leather pants, which I've paired with an oversized burgundy sweater and combat boots. "Am I not pulling off these pants?" I ask. "I know I'm not twenty-two anymore . . ."

"Please, you're rocking the pants, your ass looks fantastic, and I'm jealous, though actually, that's as good a segue as any . . ." Stephanie takes a deep breath. "You think he won't go for a girl that wears pants like that. Or dyes her hair blue. Or that doesn't want the white picket fence, and hates doing laundry, and who didn't have a My Future Wedding scrapbook when she was little . . .

"You're wrong," she continues a little more gently. "You don't see the way he looks at you. He's a man who knows what he wants, and babe, he wants you."

"Well, of course," I say with a grin. "You said it yourself. This ass in these pants . . ."

Stephanie shakes her head. "Not what I mean, and you know it. And look, I'm overstepping, I get that. We just met. But I've been where you are, I nearly missed out on the best thing in my life because I was too busy building mental checklists on all the reasons that Ethan and I wouldn't work. The thought that I could have missed out on what we have . . ."

Stephanie surprises me, reaching for my hand and giving it a squeeze. "I would be super pissed at myself if I didn't at least plant the seed that your life might not go exactly the direction you imagined—and that's okay."

"I don't imagine anything," I argue. "That's sort of the problem. I don't make plans and don't have some grand vision. He does."

"Damn," she mutters. "I've clunked it up. Okay, forget everything I've said."

She pulls me in for a quick hug, and I hug her back, even as I fight back an unfounded surge of annoyance, because she and I both know.

I won't forget what she's said. In fact, it's going to bug me the entire way home.

"Everything okay?" Thomas asks curiously, as he approaches and Stephanie runs off to where Ethan already has the car running.

"Sure. Yeah."

Thomas sees right through the lie and steps closer, concerned. "You want to talk about it? Remember," he adds, when I start to shake my head. "We're friends through the weekend, and the weekend isn't over yet. Friends tell each other crap."

I smile, but I'm not quite able to meet his eyes. Not until he gently touches his thumb to my chin, tilting my face upwards. His gray eyes are warm. Understanding. Immediately I feel some of my tension leave.

Damn it. When did this happen?

When did the one person I want to talk about become the exact same person I want to talk *to*?

"Mac?" His voice is gentle, and hearing my name jars loose a sudden desire to get in touch with the real me. The Mac who thrives on impulse and spontaneity and living in the moment, no matter how rash.

"You know that apple orchard in Connecticut?" I say. "The one you added to the 'side trip' itinerary?" I ask.

He blinks. "Sure. Yeah. I believe you described it as *super lame*?"

I press my lips together to hide my smile. "Yup. That one. Let's go there."

He looks at me for a moment, his expression lighting ever so briefly with something I can't name, and even though it's just an apple orchard, an hour out of our lives at most, I can't escape the feeling that my even asking was pivotal, and a step in the very opposite direction I intended to go.

The fact that I'm holding my breath for his answer confirms I'm very, very much in the danger zone, and should reverse *immediately*.

Then Thomas nods. Smiles. "Yeah, yeah. Let's do it."

For the life of me, I can't figure out if it's the answer I *wanted*, or if we're about to muck everything up terribly.

If the decision to stop at the apple orchard had been a mistake, it's one I'll have to deal with later, because right now? I'm pretty content to bask in the afterglow of a perfect afternoon.

The hour at the apple orchard had turned into three, though I'm not entirely sure how. One minute, I'd been planning on just snapping a few more photos of Vermont's autumn goodness and trying their "world-famous" apple cider and then getting back on the road. The next, I'd been grabbing a basket and accepting Thomas's challenge to see who could pick the most apples in an hour.

I'm still a tiny bit furious about losing—stupid short arms!—but I'd been mostly mollified by the aforementioned apple cider, which earns every bit of its world-famous label, especially when enjoyed out of a campfire mug, while sitting on a bale of hay and enumerating all the ways in which Thomas must have cheated at apple picking.

The ride home had been similarly pleasant. In fact, conversation flows so well, even if it's smattered with good-natured bickering about the best movie of all time (he goes with the cliché *Citizen Kane*, I'm an original *Ghostbusters* kind of gal), that when we get back to the city, I'm both surprised and . . . disappointed?

Thomas parks the car at the curb outside my apartment. It's raining, the downpour loud and relentless on the windshield as I unclick my seatbelt.

"Well," I say, winding my blue streak around my finger. "I don't think that's the way either of us envisioned this weekend. But we survived."

"We did. I'm sorry you couldn't spend it with Kris and his crotch V."

I laugh. It seems so long ago, both that first awkward conversation in the bar the night we met, as well as the time when a crotch V seemed important to me.

"For what it's worth," I say, turning my head all the way towards him now with a grin. "I liked *your* crotch very much."

His eyes narrow fractionally, his eyes dropping over me possessively, before he smiles. "I liked yours as well."

I force myself to open the door so that I don't do something stupid, like question why I feel so melancholy, or worse, act on it. Thomas pops the trunk and, ever the gentleman, braves the pouring rain to help me get my bags out.

I shrug on my coat and then take a bag in each hand. Before I can thank him for the ride, he steps forward, reaching out and lifting my hood to protect my face from the rain.

The pads of his thumbs brush over my cheeks, just briefly, enough that it could be an accident, though I don't think it was.

I swallow. "You're getting all wet."

He swipes at the rain in his eyes but says nothing, and I feel frantic to fill the silence that feels meaningful, somehow.

"Thanks for the ride," I say. *Crap—have I already said that?* And for . . . just, I guess, thanks," I say, feeling as out of my element as I ever have. I don't really do embarrassed, I don't do flustered, and I'm not either of those things, not really, but I am . . .

Sad.

Damn it, I'm *sad*.

"You're welcome." Thomas reaches out and slams the trunk closed. "I guess I'll . . . see you around? At the wedding?"

"Right. Yeah. Or before, if we bump into each other."

"Unavoidable for us, right?" He smiles, though it doesn't quite reach his eyes. "See you around, Mac."

I nod. "See ya."

He turns to go back to the driver's side door, but my own feet don't move.

"Thomas."

He turns, and I can't stop thinking about my conversation with Stephanie, at the possibility that I could be missing out if I don't act on this strange, unfamiliar *thing*.

"The weekend isn't over," I say in a rush. "Not technically. If you want to . . . come up?"

What am I doing?! I don't do this. I don't extend things that shouldn't be extended, I don't complicate things that should remain simple . . .

And yet my heart is in my throat anyway, hoping . . .

His eyes flick behind me towards my building, then come back to me. "I've got to return the rental car. Otherwise I'll get stuck paying for an extra day."

"Right, of course," I say, my voice a little too chipper in forced nonchalance, as I make a big deal of needlessly adjusting my grip on my bags, avoiding his eyes.

I'm relieved. I am. The ache in my chest is most definitely just embarrassment, or at least I'm pretty sure I'll be able to convince myself of it eventually.

"But," Thomas says, and my head snaps up. "I could come over after?"

The question is tentative, his voice both frustrated and almost shy, and I realize I'm not the only one utterly, totally flummoxed.

"You know—to see our friendship through the end of the weekend," he adds.

"Right. Of course. Just until midnight, when we turn into pumpkins."

He smiles. "That's not how the fairy tale goes."

I shrug. "I wouldn't know. I've never really read them, or seen the movie."

Thomas walks towards me, pressing a finger beneath my chin and pushing it gently upwards before stamping a hard kiss on my mouth.

"What was that for?" I ask, a little breathless when he pulls back.

"Let's just say I think I'm finally starting to figure you out." He looks thoughtful, pressing his finger over my bottom lip, watching the motion.

"What does *that* mean?"

"I'll let you know when I figure it out." His eyes travel back up to mine and he grins. "I'll be back here within an hour. If you don't answer the door naked, there's going to be hell to pay."

I give him a saucy smile. "What if I have something better than naked? Something black and strappy . . ."

He groans and pulls me roughly towards him for another of those delicious, claiming kisses, then sets his forehead on mine. "I don't have to return the rental car. I could risk a ticket . . . or a late fee . . . hell, to see that strappy thing, they can tow the damn thing."

I laugh and push him away. "Go. But I'll be waiting."

Only after he gets back in the car do I realize how besotted my statement must have sounded.

And worse: how besotted I actually *feel*.

CHAPTER TWENTY-ONE

Monday, October 10

The adventures of the past few weeks notwithstanding, I actually don't mind Monday mornings. I mean, I hate them the normal amount, in that they're not Friday. But usually, I'm pretty happy to be getting back to work after the weekend.

This particular Monday though, I feel unexpectedly glum. Not because I forgot to do laundry and am wearing bikini bottoms, but because I'm hungover, and not because I'm running late, but because . . .

The weekend is over. Not just any weekend: *the* weekend. The one in which I'd let myself try on an entirely different persona, became a woman who shared pizza with a guy, flirted on a bus, cuddled, and oh yeah, went apple picking.

As it turned out, Thomas and I never had to find out if we'd turned into pumpkins at midnight, because he'd left before then.

At eleven thirty-nine, to be exact. After we'd taken a long, *long* shower—together. And after we'd explored whether non-hotel sex would be as good between us as hotel sex.

God help me, though . . . it had been better. I didn't think that was possible, but sex with Thomas Decker is freaking epic and only seems to improve the more we learn each other.

Even more alarming, the casual dinner after—Greek takeout eaten sitting cross-legged on my bed—had been just as enjoyable as the hookup, though in a different way.

I don't know what is happening to me, but it's highly annoying. Even more confusing is the way I keep obsessing over the fact that he didn't mention seeing each other again.

That's *my* non-line. That's *me* who purposely doesn't commit to future hangouts, and then last night when he'd left, he hadn't said one word about the future.

I'm immensely grateful that I have a call with the agency to discuss the latest C&S campaign developments. Since Thomas's abrupt departure from the project, I've been doing his job and mine: the managing and the creative work.

Not to mention troubleshooting the nonstop barrage of Slack messages and phone calls from my team back at headquarters, who've done what they always do when the senior manager position is vacant: throw it at Mac.

It's a little overwhelming, but also pretty rewarding, and today, in particular, I'm grateful for the distraction.

I get another distraction just this afternoon when Christina stops by unannounced.

"Hey!" I tell her, dropping my headphones onto the desk and grinning at my sort-of mentor. "Coming to check up on your rogue employee?"

"Please," she says, dropping her handbag onto the chair that used to be Thomas's and pulling herself up onto the desk. "You're the most dependable employee I have." Then she laughs. "Okay, why do you look like I've just slapped you?"

I force my smile back onto my face. "No! Not at all."

She gives me a steady look, and I sigh. "Okay, fine. I guess I've always just thought of dependable as a synonym for boring."

"I get that. Not what I meant, but I get that." She leans back slightly, putting her hand on her stomach. "Ugh, my PMS is on murder-levels this month. I swear I could murder a Philly cheese-steak right now."

"We can make that happen. There's a place just around the corner that's decent."

Christina looks genuinely tempted, but then checks her watch. "I wish. I have a dental cleaning just a couple blocks over, and I'm pretty sure if I reschedule again, they'll fire me."

"I don't think dentists can fire patients."

"Sadly, you'd be wrong," she smiles. "And I actually *like* this one, because the hygienist watches all the best shows and tells me what to watch and what to skip while she cleans, but anyway." She waves her hand. "I wanted to stop by and talk in person about the senior manager position."

"Oh. Sure!"

I shouldn't be surprised. Of course I'd be getting a new boss. I've just been so consumed with the person who last had the job, as well as doing much of the job, that I haven't let myself even think about the fact that I'll have a new manager soon.

"How's the search going?" I ask. "Have you started interviewing?"

"No, I've been dragging my heels," she says with a sigh. "Especially since I apparently got it so wrong with Thomas."

I feel instantly defensive. "Thomas was a perfect hire," I say sharply, surprised by how defensive I feel. "If anything, I think the job couldn't make use of his skillset."

"I agree," she says easily. If she's surprised by my vehement defense of a boss I only had for a couple of weeks, she doesn't show it. "And you know, some of that's on me. I listened to the higher-ups' pressure to pick an Ivy Leaguer with an impeccable résumé, instead of listening to my gut."

"I'm always a fan of the gut," I say, twisting off the cap of my water bottle and taking a sip. "What's yours saying?"

"That I should offer the job to you," Christina says without preamble. "Again."

I slowly re-cap the water. "Christina—"

"I know. I know, you don't want it. But *why?* The team already looks up to you. You're easy to work with, you're exceptionally talented . . ."

She gives me a hopeful look. "Is flattery working?"

"Nope."

Christina smiles a little, but then her expression turns serious. "Look. It's your life, so I want to respect your wishes. But I also really like you, so I'm going to give this to you straight: You're coasting, Mac. You're playing it safe, and that reluctance to grow seems totally at odds with the feisty person I know. What am I missing?"

It's so spot on, I squirm a little in my seat.

"I appreciate your confidence," I say, meaning it. "But you and I have always clicked. You get me in a way that I don't know other people would if I moved up the ladder. You said it yourself, the higher-ups want an Ivy League corporate superstar who looks the part."

"So what? I have it on good authority from an Ivy League corporate superstar that my gut is right about you. That you should have the job."

"Who?" But I already know.

"Thomas. The day he gave notice, he suggested I consider hiring internally for his replacement. And he mentioned you specifically."

CHAPTER TWENTY-TWO

Monday Evening, October 10

～

I get Thomas's address from Collette. She provides it quite happily, though she also includes a smirk emoji + eggplant emoji that I choose to ignore as I walk the few blocks to his apartment.

Thomas's building is nice. Really nice. The kind of nice that makes me re-think not accepting Christina's offer today, because if *this* is what the salary affords . . .

Instead, I'd told her I need to think about it.

And before I can think about it, I have some *words* for Thomas Decker.

His building has a doorman, two of them, actually, so I have to wait impatiently while a nice guy named Van calls Thomas.

"You're all good!" Van says with a smile as he hangs up the phone. "Go on up. Twelfth floor."

Thomas's expression is surprised when he answers my knock, and maybe a little wary. "Hey."

"Hey," I snap, pushing past him into his apartment, and stare around accusingly, looking for something not to like. There's plenty.

It's . . . pristine.

The counter tops are some sort of white stone, the utensil holder is sleek stainless steel, the stovetop is streak free. His laptop is open, and even that's perfect, I bet he's never touched it with Cheez-It fingers or known the panic of spilling a bit of coconut La Croix on the track pad.

The couch is some sort of gray, textured fabric that looks both expensive and comfortable, the coffee table is concrete and perfect, and . . .

Okay fine, it's not that bad.

I whirl on him. "I got a job offer today."

He says nothing.

"A promotion. And you're not surprised," I continue. "Because you were the one to suggest it."

He shrugs. "So? You told me yourself Christina had offered you the position. All I did was tell her that her instincts were right."

"That wasn't your place!"

"Yes, it was, Mac," he says.

He says it calmly. So calmly that my fists clench, because I'm in the mood to fight, for some reason, and he's being all *reasonable*.

"I may have only been your boss for two weeks, but I *was* your boss," he continued, "I gave it my very best, and ironically, part of being successful in that particular role meant realizing that I wasn't the best person for the job. It took me all of two days of speaking with the team to realize that you were the best person for the job.

"And wait," he says, holding up a hand with a quick shake of his head. "Are you here because you're *mad* at me? Because I recommended you for a promotion?"

"You recommended me *after* I told you I didn't want it." I cross my arms, feeling defensive. "It's like you thought you knew what was better for me than I did."

I'm expecting—wanting—an apology for his high-handedness, but he doesn't give it to me. Instead, he shrugs. "Maybe in this case, I do."

My mouth drops open. "How—"

"We all need someone to encourage us to grow, and you don't have that person, Mac. You're the clear alpha in your relationship with Collette, your team would jump through hoops to do as you say, and it's clearly not going to be your mom who pushes you out of your comfort zone—"

"Stop. You do not get to weigh in on my relationship with my mother because you've met her *once*."

"I'm not. I just—" He looks frustrated. "If you don't want to be a senior manager—"

"I don't," I interrupt.

"Right. Got it. If you don't want to be a senior manager, that's obviously your call, but don't settle, Mac."

"Just because my life plan doesn't mimic yours doesn't mean it's *settling*."

My response seems to nudge his frustration towards fed up, because his eyes flash angrily and he crosses his arms. "You clearly have no interest in hearing anything I have to say, so why are you here?"

I swallow, and because my work backpack is increasingly heavy

on my shoulders, I shrug it off and set it on the floor, before dropping onto his couch. I cross my arms over my stomach, feeling a
little defensive. A lot confused.

Thomas comes and sits beside me. Close, but not touching.
Comforting, somehow, even though I sense he's still frustrated.

"I don't want it," I say in a low voice.

"That's fine." He moves as though to take my hand, then seems
to think better of it. "It's not for everyone. Take it from the guy
who quit."

I shift towards him. "You know when I accepted Elodie's offer,
it was supposed to be a six-month gig? I'd just gotten evicted—
evicted, Thomas—because I was careless with the freelance
business I was so gung ho about, spending more than I made . . .

"Then six months turned into a year. And then . . . I'm still
there, and they want more from me, more commitment,
and . . . that's not me. I'm not someone who makes plans."

"Sure you do," he says quietly. "You make plans not to make
plans. In a lot of ways, you're the most deliberate person I know."

I scowl at him. "Take that back!"

"Ah," he says, very softly. "I see what's going on here."

"Do you?" I ask with a sharp laugh. "Because I don't."

"You're not mad at me," Thomas says.

"Oh, believe me, I am."

"No. You're not. You're mad at yourself, because a part of
you—I don't know how big or small—is considering the job
Christina offered. And you're *furious*. You're mad because it
doesn't gel with the Mac you want to be, the Mac that you think
you are."

I try to stand, but he grips my hand, forcing me to stay seated, to meet his gray eyes. "It's okay to change, Mac. To evolve. To blow up the ideal of your life and build another one. Circumstances are always changing, we're allowed to change along with them."

He's right. On some level, I know he's right, and it makes me furious, both because it's uncomfortable to hear, and because he seems to be reading me better than I can read myself.

"What if I were to take it—hypothetically," I say, a touch desperately. "What if I were to take it and get stuck? What if I wake up one day and I'm fifty, still at the same company, working with the same people?"

"What if you are?"

The question is so simple, so drama-free and gently delivered that it seems to pierce through a bubble I didn't fully realize I was living in.

And on the other side of that bubble, I see a billion different paths that my life could take, and all of them would be . . . fine. Just fine. Some could even be great. But I won't know if I don't try.

"Look." He takes my hand for real this time. "You're strong-willed to the point of being absolutely infuriating. Nobody can make you do a damn thing you don't want to. And you can always change it up again, at any time, as often as you want to. Take the job. Ditch the job. It doesn't matter. You're still Mac. You're still you."

I swallow and look into his eyes that are so confident, so sure of me, that I want . . . I want . . .

For the second time in a month, I'm sitting on a couch and lean forward to press my mouth against Thomas Decker's.

It's a different couch, and with different results. His response to my kiss is immediate. This time he kisses me back, his mouth warm and firm and reassuring.

"The weekend's over," I whisper.

"I know," he says, sliding a hand into my hair and pulling my face closer.

"It was supposed to be a one-time thing. I still don't want to be your girlfriend."

"I know." His mouth trails over my jaw, down my neck, and I let my head fall back.

"And I—"

He pulls back with a rueful grin. "You're not going to start talking about my mother again, are you?"

I laugh. "No. No, trust me, I am not thinking about Mary in this moment."

I am, however, thinking a little bit about my own mother, about her reaction if I tell her that I took the job. Or worse, that I might be falling, big time, for a guy . . .

And I don't want to think about that. Not now. My hands fist in Thomas's hair, a little desperately, and he understands. He must understand, because he takes my hand once more and tugs me to my feet.

He reaches up, runs a thumb along my blue streak, smiling as he looks down at me. "Shall we try my bed? Maybe it's the one that lets us down . . ."

"It would be irresponsible not to do our due diligence," I say with a somber face.

"My thoughts exactly."

CHAPTER TWENTY-THREE

Tuesday Evening, October 11

~

"This doesn't look right—does it?" I ask Thomas the next evening, tilting the mixing bowl in his direction.

He gives the tan-colored goo a dubious look. "It looks sort of . . . crumbly."

"It says right here," I say, picking up my phone to read off the apple pie recipe. "Do not overmix. Dough should resemble pebbles."

"Well, if your idea of pebbles is sand, you're on the right track," he says.

I look at the bowl contents and sigh. He's not wrong. It looks like sand.

I thrust the bowl at him and pick up my wine glass. "You fix it."

"Why me?"

"You're the domesticated one," I say reasonably. "Some day you're going to be hosting holidays, and I *know* you're not going to be one of those guys who thinks his wife should be doing all the cooking and baking."

"No," he says, "I'm not. I'm one of those guys that thinks that store-bought pie is just fine. And for all your accusations that I'm the domesticated one, baking apple pie was *your* suggestion."

"What else were we supposed to do with all those apples!" I protest. "Plus, it was just my idea to try and make a pie. Your idea to do it here at your place."

And for reasons I'm choosing not to contemplate at this moment, I hadn't just agreed, I'd actually happily agreed. In fact, if I'm going to be all the way honest, my heart had done a happy little squeeze when he'd suggested it.

"Because when I asked if you have a mixing bowl, measuring cup, measuring spoons, pie dish—"

I hold up a finger. "Hey. You didn't have one of those either."

"Easily remedied." Thomas lifts the pie dish that still has the sticker and bar code on it from when we'd picked it up from the bodega. "But I had everything else."

"Not that you've used any of it," I say, settling onto a bar stool and helping myself to more wine. "What did you do, buy some sort of kitchen starter kit when you moved in?"

He blinks. "Yes. Doesn't everybody?"

I smile. *Adorable.* "No. Not everyone. But I'm glad you did. Now I can taste-test the pie you're about to finish making with all your fancy equipment."

"You're lucky you're cute," he mutters, as he lifts a measuring cup that we've filled with ice water, per recipe suggestion. "What do you think? More water?"

"It certainly can't hurt!" I say cheerfully.

"Uh huh," he says, pouring a little drizzle into the bowl and beginning to massage it into the dough. "If you're done offering up such helpful bits of advice, how do you feel about peeling apples?"

"I feel like that sounds relatively straightforward." I set my glass aside after another sip. "Where's the peeler?"

"No clue," he says, nodding with his chin towards the drawers. "Try one of those."

I find it after a bit of rummaging around, and grabbing another bowl, I come to stand beside him and begin peeling as he curses the dough.

My motions are slow at first—ordering a pizza on my phone is way easier than actually having to work for my own food—but eventually I gain a bit of confidence, my motions becoming faster and more efficient.

Thomas, too, seems to be having a bit of luck. He tilts the bowl my way. "These are pebbles, right?"

I lean down, inspecting, and grin. "Pebbles!"

"Now to turn pebbles into crust," he says, upending the bowl and forming it into a mound. "Remind me again how you ended up with the easy part and I got this?"

"Because you love a challenge."

"Apparently," he mutters, rather cryptically.

We work in companionable silence for several moments, pausing only when he says, "wine me," so I can lift his wine glass to his mouth, since his hands are covered in flour.

I can't resist sneaking a few peeks as he painstakingly rolls out the uncooperative dough. Had somebody told me a month ago that I'd be lusting over a clean-cut guy holding a rolling pin, with his white dress shirt rolled up to his elbows, I'd have laughed in their face.

Now, here I am, getting a little hot and bothered wishing he had a manly looking apron to complete the look.

Who am I?

Finally, in what probably takes way longer than it should, he has the bottom crust adequately, if not prettily, in the pie dish, and I have a bowl of cinnamon and nutmeg flavored sliced apples that I carefully dump onto the dough.

"Now for what I have to imagine is the hard part," he says, nodding at the awkwardly rolled out top crust.

I swipe at my forehead with the back of my hand. "Go for it."

"Uh uh. Together."

"This isn't a corporate retreat where we have to pump up the importance of teamwork. It doesn't take two people to make a pie."

"Obviously, it does," he says with a quick smile. "But no, we're *both* doing this, because then we'll both have the satisfaction of victory when this piece of shit comes out of the oven."

I laugh, because the combination of romanticism and impatience pretty much sums up so much of what I like about him.

I shrug, and carefully peel up the other side of the dough. We probably could have done it with one person, but a double-crusted pie is no joke for one's first attempt, so it's sort of nice to have company in making a hash out of it.

After watching a quick YouTube video showing us how to "crimp the crust together," we each start at opposite sides and work our way around the dish until we have what can only be described as a train wreck, but it's our train wreck.

He lifts a palm, and I smack it in a high-five, the gesture sending flour everywhere, which I'd have thought would upset his tidy little world, but instead of seeming annoyed, he lowers his head and kisses me.

I kiss him back, sighing a little at the realization that the sheer pleasure of something as simple as kissing this man hasn't abated even though we keep doing it, even though we're doing it on a random Tuesday at home, instead of confining it to a sexy "what happens in Vermont stays in Vermont" weekend as planned.

Thomas pulls back. "Did you preheat the oven?"

I think back. Shoot. "I *meant* to. Does that count?"

He smiles, and after checking the recipe, pushes some buttons on the oven to turn it on.

"Now we have to wait for it to come up to temp and bake? That'll take forever," I say with a touch of whining.

"It's just as well." He checks his watch. "You can't have pie for dinner."

"Says who?"

He opens his mouth. "Fair point. But I know I for one would like some actual dinner first. Especially since we don't know how that will turn out."

He points skeptically at our pie, which, I'll admit, looks absolutely nothing like the picture.

"Alright," I sigh. "I'll get out of your hair and let you be an adult, but don't you dare eat all the pie. You leave my half with your doorman for me to pick up tomorrow after work, or else."

I draw a line across my throat before finishing the last bit of wine and reaching for my work bag on the floor beside his dining table.

"Wait." Thomas reaches out and grabs my hand. "Stay."

I give him a look. "For dinner? I can't."

"Why not?"

My look is even more pointed this time. "You know why I can't."

"Explain it to me in your weird Mac words."

"It's too coupley."

"And baking a pie together isn't?"

"That was different. Practical," I say, trying to ignore how stupid my argument sounds. "We had to use up the apples."

He reaches out a hand and touches my blue streak, something I notice he does often, though not, as I first thought, as a way of reminding himself how ill-suited we are. It feels almost affectionate, as though he's relishing the fact that I let him do it instead of batting his hand away.

And then, to remind myself who I am, and what I'm not, I bat his hand away.

But the damn man only smiles, knowingly. "Look. We've tried things your way. We put up the walls, we put up the time limits, we set all sorts of boundaries. It didn't work."

"Don't even think about suggesting we try things your way," I say, eyes wide with panic. "Just because I make one pie with you—"

"I was going to suggest a compromise," he interrupts. "We keep doing whatever this is. Hanging out if we feel like it. Having sex if we feel like it. Even staying over if we feel like it."

My heart clenches in panic. "That sounds an awful lot like your way." *An awful lot like a relationship.*

"I'm not done." He steps closer and slides his arms around my waist, casually. "I was going to add that we do this just for as long as it suits us. Because I like spending time with you, perhaps against my better judgment, and you like spending time with me."

"I—"

He kisses me, slow and tongue-twisting and promising.

"Fine," I say, when he pulls back. "I like spending time with you *a little*."

His eyes crinkle at the corners in an almost smile. "All I'm suggesting is that if it feels good, we should do it and I'm not just talking about the sex. I like apple picking with you. I even like pie-baking with you. And talking. And arguing. You can call it friends-with-benefits, or don't call it anything at all, I don't really care."

"How is this not a boyfriend/girlfriend situation?" I ask skeptically.

He thinks this over. "Because if you want to walk away, at any point, you can. No breakup speech, no fear of hurting me, or pressure to stay longer than you want to in the name of commitment."

"And we don't have to be exclusive. We can sleep with other people?" I ask, a wild defensive swing if I've ever felt one.

His jaw tenses a little, and his nod is short. "Yes. If you want to sleep with someone else you should feel free to."

He sucks in his cheeks slightly and meets my eyes. "Just like if I want to sleep with someone else, I won't hesitate."

I don't recognize the feeling that hits me in the stomach just then. Irritation? Anger? Pain?

None of those, I realize. It's a new one for me, and as awful as all the songs and movies make it out to be:

Jealousy.

To say that it's unpleasant would be an understatement, but another realization is just as jarring as how much I don't want to even think about him with someone else:

It's that I don't want to be with anyone else either.

CHAPTER TWENTY-FOUR

Tuesday, October 18

~

A week later, I'm bursting with news. Good news, big news, the kind that I'd normally go straight to my mom or Collette with.

Instead, I find myself calling Thomas's cell as I step out of the Elodie headquarters and walk the couple of streets over to Central Park. *Calling*, not even texting. I recognize myself a little less every day, and yet at the same time, I feel more myself than ever.

"Is it done?" he says after the first ring.

"It's final. I just signed."

"Hell yes!" he says with heartfelt enthusiasm. "I told you they'd go for your counter offer!"

I hadn't taken the senior manager position that Christina offered. In fact, I'd been quite blunt in telling them that I didn't think it should even *be* a position.

There was a reason that nobody stayed in the role for more than six months, with Thomas's case being the most extreme, but not the first:

That person doesn't have anything to do other than babysit us creative types, and I'll be the first to admit that we can be a little eccentric and delicate-flower when it comes to our work. But the company was making a misstep every time they prioritized bringing in someone with management experience instead of design experience.

Granted, I as a designer myself would have been a step in the right direction, but I also didn't want to give up something I loved (designing) in exchange for sitting in meetings all day with no actual deliverables. Not only for my own sake, but after six years on this team, I know it's also not what the team needs.

To say nothing of the fact that the position had to be downright miserable, because it was essentially a glorified go-between. More often than not, even when there was someone in the position, Christina had gone straight to myself, or to Layla or Sadie, the next two senior members for quicker results.

So I suggested an alternate structure. Instead of stepping into the shoes of *Senior Manager, Web Design*, I proposed a brand new role altogether: Director of Digital Strategy.

That's right. I went from not sure I wanted a promotion at all to suggesting they bump me up *two* levels, which would put me on the same tier as Christina.

And this is where I owe Thomas big time, because he'd walked me through how to position the proposal. Not just with a new position and a promotion for me, but a new position and a promotion for Christina, who would become *senior* director of web marketing.

It would free Christina up from the day-to-day grit of our team, which I knew she would like. It freed me up to deliver an actual something—*strategy*—and also do what I'd loved so much about the C&S side project, liaising with third parties, and looking at the Elodie online presence as it presents on the entire web, not just our internal website.

And, as one last little twist, instead of eight direct reports, I'll only have three, with Sadie taking on a new position as manager of the copyediting team, and Layla, manager of the graphic design team.

Honestly? I hadn't been holding my breath. It had all seemed like too much. Or maybe I hadn't held my breath because I was aware I wanted it just a tiny bit too much and had wanted to mitigate the disappointment.

But they'd gone for it. I'd presented the idea to Christina yesterday afternoon. She'd taken it to her leadership this morning. And . . .

It's happening.

It's actually happening.

"How do you feel?" Thomas asks, and I sort of adore him for asking, for understanding that this is one hell of a pivot for me.

"I feel . . . really good," I say, with a happy laugh. "I'm surprised to hear myself say it, honestly. Last week, a promotion sounded like my worst nightmare—"

"That promotion," Thomas corrects. "That promotion wasn't right. This one is. Sometimes the perfect fit comes from discovering something we didn't know existed. Could exist."

"That's very deep," I say, intentionally keeping my voice teasing, because I'm pretty sure there's a chance he's not just talking about my new job. And I'm not ready to think about that, much less talk about it.

"How about we celebrate?" he asks, letting me off the hook. "Or is it too early?"

"Christina told me to head out, go relish my last few days as Mac Austin, senior web designer. So heck yes, take me somewhere nice!"

"Settle down, Ms. Director, remember only one of us is employed," he says dryly.

"Don't worry, we'll find something just as amazing for you!" I say, then bite my lip, as I realize now *I'm* the one saying we, and that I'm referring to the future.

Thomas, perhaps wisely, doesn't touch that one, and suggests meeting up at a swanky cocktail bar overlooking Central Park.

It's one of those fancy places that's totally not my style, but today, it feels right, as does the expensive bottle of champagne that Thomas orders.

Over drinks, he lets me ramble on about my ideas, chiming in with several of his own.

"Okay, enough about me," I say, after our glasses have been topped off. "I've been dominating conversation all day. No, all week."

"That's alright. It's what I'm—I haven't minded."

It's what I'm here for.

I'm almost positive that's what he'd intended to say and had bit it back, and I know why he bit it back. It's because the mere suggestion of relying on him in any meaningful way makes me jumpy as hell.

Pushing past the thought, I nudge his knee with mine. "Okay, for real though. What about you? The life of leisure is still treating you well?"

"Actually, no," he says with a laugh. "Yesterday I was so bored with myself that I considered making another pie."

"Oof," I say. "That you would even want to *think* about a repeat of Pie Pile . . ."

Our apple pie had been a messy disaster. Tasty, to be sure. We'd managed to eat the entire thing within twenty-four hours. But pretty it was not. I'm not even sure it could be called pie, hence our revised label for the dessert: Pie Pile. As in a pile of crumbled crust and fruit.

"I know. I guess I felt I needed the challenge." He says it distractedly as he fishes one of the bar nuts out of the tiny bowl they'd placed in front of us. I watch him carefully, because there had been something in his tone just then . . .

"You have a plan," I say, because apparently I can read him now. It's like I just . . . know. "You've figured out what you want to do—where you want to apply to?"

Thomas hesitates. "This is your celebration. You deserve to hog all the attention."

"I'm done hogging, I want to hear about what you're doing next. It can't be a director, because I just finally got the upper hand on you, but I'll support just about anything else," I say with a smile. "Oh, and I can make your résumé look good. I'll bet yours is a Times New Roman disaster."

"Well, actually, I was thinking maybe *not* going the résumé route."

"Is that even possible?" I ask curiously. "I'm not exactly a conformist, but even I know most companies want a résumé."

"I don't think I want to join a company. I think I want to start one. Try my hand at being a freelancer."

My mouth drops open. "Has the world turned upside down?

I'm going all-in on a big company, and *you're* going the scrappy entrepreneur route?"

"Well, I'm not going to put on a beanie and start working out of my parents' garage just yet."

"Knowing you, you'll probably wear a suit just to go to work at your kitchen table."

He frowns, and I set a finger to his mouth. "For the record, I think that's hot. For as much time as you spent in a suit during our early days, it's a crime that I haven't had the pleasure of getting you out of one yet."

I actually don't think I've *ever* gone to bed with a man wearing a suit—it's always been the exact opposite of my type. And yet, now it's all I can think about. Tugging at the tie. Easing the jacket over broad male shoulders . . .

Not any tie, not any shoulders. Thomas. Just Thomas.

"So what's the business idea?" I ask, when the vibe between us feels a little too charged.

"To start, just me as a freelancer. A project manager. I'm good at it. No, I'm great at it. And most companies who rely on their FTE headcount for project managers have a hard time because it's vital for PMs to stay out of internal politics, and when they are internal, they can't help but get pulled in."

I nod in agreement. "Very true—it's rare to sit through a meeting about workload assignment that isn't rife either with turf wars, or offloading the crap jobs to another team."

"Exactly. But if it's a freelancer, someone who's just there for the project and nothing else, I can assign and reassign tasks without bias, and they can feel free to hate me without turning on each other."

"That sounds terrible, and I think you'll be perfect at it," I grin.

He grins back. "It's early stages yet. I'm barely out of brain-storming, but I already have at least one client who's interested."

"Yeah?"

"Yup." He tosses an almond into his mouth and chews. "This jewelry brand I worked for. I was only there two weeks, but I think I made an impression."

"Did you now," I say with a smile as I realize he's talking about Elodie. "Are you sure it was a *good* impression?"

"Oh, I'm quite sure. It was not a good impression. But I've done some damage control, and I think I've reversed early opinions."

I narrow my eyes. "You are talking about Christina as your in, right? Because if it's me, I won't have enough pull early on, it would take some time."

"Mac, Mac, Mac. You do realize you're proposing *quite* the potential conflict of interest? Bringing on a freelancer who's also your lover?"

"Ugh, use the word 'lover' again and we won't be conflicting our interests ever again." Then I wiggle my eyebrows. "That said, when I signed on to be a director, I never promised no scandals."

"Much appreciated," he laughs. "But I was actually referring to Christina as my in. She said to let her know if I ever decided to go the contract route; apparently it's a path they're exploring for project management, especially on things like the C&S campaign."

"Huh." I take a distracted sip of champagne.

"That okay?" he asks.

"Of course! I guess I'm just realizing it means that I could see you on a regular basis even as long as you and I are no longer doing this." I gesture between us.

He watches me carefully. "You're not freaking out about that?"

I'm cautious with my answer. "We're adults. I have no doubt that we'll be able to be civil long after we stop sleeping together."

"And when you learn, someday, that I'm seeing someone, how will you feel about that?"

My stomach tightens. "Are you?"

"Not currently. But I will, someday, Mac. I'm looking for someone to share my life with. You know that."

I do know that. And I know I have to respect it just like he respects I don't want that. I do respect it, I want Thomas to be happy.

It's just that I also sort of *hate* how much I hate the Future Mrs. Decker.

CHAPTER TWENTY-FIVE

Thursday, October 20

～

*M*y mom's apartment is not one of those "places you can go home to." For starters, it's always changing. As when I was growing up and we rarely stayed in the same place for more than a year, my mother is leaning more towards vagabond than ever.

She'll find a "great little place just off the L train," that she'll stay in six months, tops, before she inevitably ends up sleeping on her friend Debbie's couch again, because "it just didn't work out."

My couch is no stranger to her nomad ways as well, and though I love her, that's way too much togetherness, so I've found a gentle but effective way of limiting that particular routine. It's as simple as telling her of course she can stay at my place, as long as she wants, and then after (noisily) making my coffee before work every morning, asking my mother, who'd clearly wanted to sleep until noon, in my most chipper voice:

"What are your plans for the day?"

It's a good strategy, if I do say so myself. Even my wonderfully loopy mother doesn't like having to answer "nothing" more than three days in a row, which ensures her stay is always short.

I used to feel a little guilty about not encouraging her to stay longer until Collette helped me reframe: by not allowing my mom to sleep on my couch indefinitely, it preserved our relationship. Because no mother–daughter relationship, no matter how stable, needs that kind of proximity.

And you know, my relationship with my mom? It's good. She drives me crazy. A lot. Sometimes I wish she were just a tiny bit more traditional, in the sense that I could lean on her.

But I've accepted that she is who she is, and we are what we are.

One of the best parts of having the "fun mom" is our happy-hour tradition. We're both always on the lookout for the best deals, the kind of place that has not just fifty-cent wings on Wednesday, but prime rib sliders and martinis, not just generic "well drinks." My latest find is a new Mexican place, with three-dollar shrimp tacos, and pretty great margaritas.

"So," Mom says as she painstakingly picks cilantro off her taco and sets it on the rim of her plate. "I've been dying of curiosity, what is your big news that you refused to tell me over text?

"No, no, I want to guess," she says before I can answer, settling more firmly on her bar stool. "You've discovered the best sex of your life."

"Mom!"

"What!" she protests. "I thought I raised you never to think of sex or female pleasure as a sin."

"I don't, I just think discussing it with my mother is."

The noise she makes is indignant. "Okay, fine. So, not sex, at least not that you'll talk to me about," she says, tapping her nails as she considers an alternate reason for why I'd want to celebrate.

"You haven't changed your hair," she muses, looking me over, and I have to smile, because in her mind that really would be reason to celebrate.

"New job!" she says, tapping the bar in victory at her guess. "I know it."

"Ding ding ding," I say, smiling and raising a glass.

She clinks hers to mine, grinning. "A mother always knows. And let me just say, it's about damn time. I can tell you now that you're moving on, you were turning into a downright fuddy-duddy working at the same company for years on end. I was half expecting you to start wearing shoulder pads and talking about a stock portfolio."

She's busy giving a dramatic shudder, so she misses the fact that my smile has frozen on my face.

"Actually," I say slowly, setting my glass aside. "The new job is with the same company. A promotion. A big one," I can't help adding.

"Oh! *Oh!*"

She looks . . . disappointed. She tries to hide it, but it's there, and it stings.

"Well, if that's what you want, that's great," she says, taking a bite of her taco.

"It is," I say, a touch testily. "It's a big deal, actually."

"Of course it is." She wipes her mouth and smiles. "You're making more money, right? That's never a bad thing."

Not for you. The thought is a little bitchy, but I can't help it. I can practically see the wheels turning in her head as she realizes a silver lining of having a fuddy-duddy daughter: more money for her to "borrow."

Testing the theory, I grab a tortilla chip, dunk it in salsa, and ask casually, "Hey, I've been so wrapped up in my own stuff, I never even asked: How's that VA class going?"

"Oh, that." She waves her hand. "Turns out it wasn't for me."

"But you were so excited about it!"

"I guess a break from straightening treatments and trimming split ends sounded pretty great, but I realized pretty quickly that a life spent behind a computer screen all day is no life at all. No offense."

"No, yeah, of course not. Why would I take offense at that? It's not like you just described my life or anything."

"Oh, sweetie. I didn't mean it like that! It's just not for *me*. I've realized I need to do something that allows me to move around, talk to people face-to-face and really help them, you know?"

I nod in resignation, because I know a lead-up when I hear one.

"Do you think I'd make a good physical therapist?" she continues. "All my clients say I'm so easy to talk to, so I think my sympathy could be a real asset. And I've always been such a big proponent of staying physically active. Last night I was grabbing a bite out at a bar, and this guy next to me—*really* good looking—was telling me that he used to be a bartender and made great money, but that the hours sucked, so he went to school to be a PT, and now his quality of life is way better."

Don't ask. Don't ask. Don't ask. Do not ask how much the school is.

I stay strong. I don't ask. But she tells me anyway.

"It's just that the program is so expensive, you know? But a really good investment, especially when you think of all the good I could do . . ."

"Mom . . ."

"Oh, honey, no, that wasn't a hint," she says with a scandalized laugh, as though the very thought of me loaning her money is ludicrous. "Just venting a little is all. I'll figure out a way to pay for it, it'll just take some sacrifices is all."

I blow out a breath. "I want to support you. I really do, I just . . ."

"You're tired of throwing money away when I don't stick with anything?"

I flinch, but she sets a hand on my knee, squeezes. "Don't. You're absolutely right, and I'm proud of you for standing up to me."

I'm a little stunned, because my mom doesn't get real like that. Not very often, and not about money, and her own shortcomings, but before I can reply, she's right back to her usual Annette self.

"So." She leans in. "You won't give me the deets on the sex. But will you at least tell your old mom about the guy who's given you that glow? I know that look, and no job, no matter how great the paycheck, can cause it."

I have to smile a little at that, because for all her quirks, and she has plenty, she can read me the way only a mom can.

And I smile too, because thinking about Thomas does that.

"He's just this guy, who's . . . he's all wrong for me," I say in a rush. "Just, my pure opposite, everything I thought would bore me to death, but he's also just really *good*, you know? I feel good when I'm with him."

"That's the sex," Mom says with a smirk, then quickly mimes zipping her lips and throwing away the key. "Oops."

"It's not just the sex," I admit slowly, trying the words on for size, half expecting lightning to strike.

I take a big breath for courage. "Mom, did you ever . . . has there ever been a guy where you thought you could be really happy with him? Not just for right now, not just in bed, but like, forever?"

"Oh sure," she says with a laugh.

"Really?" My mom is the poster child for love 'em and leave 'em.

"Of course!" She licks some of the salt off her margarita rim. "When I was young and stupid. It's all part of growing up, baby girl."

My heart sinks. "Young and stupid."

"Not stupid," she amends quickly. "That's not what I meant. It's just . . . one of those things that you learn as you get older. When you're a kid, you eventually discover there's no Santa Claus. When you're an adult, you discover there's no Prince Charming. It's bitter-sweet at first, but eventually you just sort of smile at the things young-you believed and accept things as they are."

"And how are they?"

"They're . . ." She waves her hand. "Transient. Evolving. That's the fun of it, baby girl. Enjoy this man you're with—Thomas, is it? The man I met at your apartment?"

I blink. "How did you know?"

"Because I saw the way he looked at you. Like you intrigued the heck out of him. And he did the same for you. I get it! All that sexy, buttoned-up charisma. I had a guy like that once. Andy something or other."

"What happened?" I ask, because I've heard about lots of her guys, and Andy doesn't ring a bell.

"We enjoyed each other wildly. He loved my spontaneity, I loved his credit card," she says with a laugh. "Last I checked on Facebook, he was happily married to a woman—a real estate broker—living in New Jersey with three kids, and commuting to the city, exactly as he should be. And I'm having tequila with my daughter on a Wednesday night, exactly as I should be."

"I don't want to be a real estate broker in Jersey," I say, mostly to myself.

My mom squeezes my hand. "Of course you don't. But that doesn't mean you can't enjoy what you and Thomas have while it's still good. The key is letting it go before it starts to turn on you."

I look at her, needing maternal advice like never before. "But how do you know? How do you know when it's about to turn?"

"Practice," she says with a wink. "But my advice? The second it stops feeling good, when it starts to feel complicated instead of easy-breezy, that's your cue to gracefully bow out. At the end of the day, it's the kindest thing we can do for someone else—letting them go before things turn ugly."

Later that night, I'm curled up in Thomas's bed, my head on his shoulder, my conversation with my mom doing perfect, relentless figure eights inside my head.

It's the kindest thing we can do for someone else—letting them go before things turn ugly . . .

It had made perfect sense in the moment, but now I'm wishing

I would have asked her a bit more about knowing when they were about to turn. She'd said *practice*, but I don't want Thomas to be practice. I just want him to be . . . mine.

Just a little bit longer.

Thomas's breathing is slow and rhythmic, the way it is when he sleeps, so I'm surprised when he slides a hand over my bare back, his lips brushing against the top of my head in a kiss. "You want to talk about it?"

"About what?" I wince at the flippancy in my tone, at my knee-jerk reaction to keep him at emotional arm's length, even when I'm happy to turn over every inch of my physical self.

He doesn't answer my reflexive question, nor does he push. He just waits, steady and . . . *there*.

I lift my head. "I hung out with my mom today."

"Oh yeah?"

I nod. "Just before I came over here."

Neither of us mentions the fact that I am here. It hadn't been planned. In fact, I'd specifically told Thomas I had other plans tonight. And yet, when I'd left happy hour, my feet had turned here rather than home. And when he'd opened his front door, there had been no surprise, no question, no hesitation.

He'd been eating popcorn and watching re-runs of some cop show, so that's what I'd done as well. It was the sort of evening my nightmares were once made out of, a couple so boring they spent all night plopped on the couch, barely speaking. And yet it hadn't felt like a nightmare at all.

It had felt like a slice of *real life*, the kind of little moments that add up to big ones when you're not looking.

Thomas hadn't asked me to stay over, nor had I asked to.

Somehow we'd just found ourselves in his bed, and instead of reaching for each other with restless, eager hands, Thomas had pulled me close, as though understanding that I was all up in my head and I needed a chance to sort my thoughts.

It's the first time we've gone to bed without sex, and instead of feeling worried, it feels like another of those pivotal moments—a warning sign that this has become about something bigger than sexual release.

I rub my chin against his chest hair. "Do you think I'm a fuddy-duddy?"

He lets out a quiet laugh. "You're a lot of things, Mac. That's not a word I'd use for you."

I tilt my head up and find him watching me steadily. "But am I getting boring? With the new job, and . . ." *You?*

His hand rubs over my hair, the thumb gliding on the blue. "You told her about your promotion?"

"Mm hmm." I don't elaborate on her reaction, but from his slight frown, I'm pretty sure he knows.

"I liked your mom, the time I met her," he says after a moment.

"But?" I smile.

"*And,*" he says, smiling back. "She struck me as a woman who is very clear on who she is, and who likes who she is. That's a rare thing, and a good thing."

"*Now* the but," I joke.

"But," Thomas says, his arm pulling me a bit closer. "I wonder if maybe she isn't so enamored with her way of life as the best way that it hasn't occurred to her to let you form your own vision of what Mac wants."

I shake my head. "She's always been very into encouraging me to follow my own passions, not hers. It's why I got into design, when she has no interest in that whatsoever."

"Just because you forged your own career path doesn't mean she wasn't making you into a, uh, let's say *Mini-Me* in other ways."

"She didn't *make* me anything," I say defensively. "We've just always been cut from the same cloth."

Thomas says nothing. He doesn't have to. The gap of silence does it for him, forcing me to sit with some uncomfortable thoughts, to reframe some old memories, to reassess . . .

Me.

"My life was simpler before I met you," I say, even as I stroke a finger over his jawline, grateful for his quiet nearness.

"Mine too," he says quietly. "More boring though."

"I thought you liked boring."

"I did. But maybe you're not the only one rethinking some things."

I want to ask him what, but I'm too terrified that the answer will change everything. Too terrified that everything's already changing.

Wanting a distraction, needing it, needing him, I slide a leg over his and shift positions until instead of lying beside him, I'm lying atop him, my legs straddling his hips.

"Reassure me," I say quietly, running my hands up his chest, over the undershirt he's sleeping in. "Reassure me I'm not a boring fuddy-duddy."

"Well, now," he murmurs, his hands sliding to my panty-clad ass, pulling me a bit further against his already growing erection. "It seems to me that a *non* fuddy-duddy would go to bed topless, and yet here you are, in one of my T-shirts."

"Hmm." I look down at the gray Dartmouth shirt I'd commandeered for the evening. "I guess I'll have to take it off?"

"I think that's probably best," he says, with fake regret.

I take my time, easing the shirt upwards, halting the process just below my breasts, relishing the look of eagerness on his face before I tug it over my head, let it drop to the side.

"How about this?" I say, running a finger along the side of my breast, highlighting their nakedness. "Better?"

"A little," he says hoarsely. "You still seem a bit reserved though."

"Reserved, hmm." I scoot up and lean forward slowly, positioning my breast just in front of his mouth. "And now?"

"Better." His breath is hot on the tip of my breast, and I arch just a tiny bit, letting my nipple brush against his mouth.

Thomas lets out a tortured groan, his tongue giving my nipple a single teasing lick because his hand slides between my shoulder blades, pulling me all the way to him so his lips can close around me.

He sucks hard and I gasp, my hands bracing on either side of his head as he sucks on one breast, then the other, using his teeth to tease them into hard, aching peaks.

I feel a finger teasing around the edge of my underwear, slipping just under and then retreating, getting me wetter and wetter until finally a finger slips all the way beneath. Inside.

I cry out, and sit up, the position allowing him to slide a second finger inside me as he looks up at me with hot, silver eyes. "Show me," he says. "Show me how unabashed you can be."

I lift my hips slowly, then lower them, sinking all the way onto his fingers as we both groan. I repeat the process, again, my pace quickening until I'm completely lost.

His other hand slips beneath the top of my panties, easing them aside with a thumb that he presses over my clit with the exact right pressure, the perfect rhythm, and my orgasm catches me by surprise, my body tightening around his fingers as I arch my back with a loud, uninhibited scream of pleasure.

I stay that way for a long moment, gasping for breath, waiting for the stars to recede before looking back at him, my expression smug. "I don't think a fuddy-duddy would have ridden someone's hand."

"Probably not," he concedes, as he eases me off his hips and opens his nightstand drawer for a condom. "But let's just run one last test . . ."

Thomas tugs my underwear down my legs with a roughness that turns me on all over again, but when I start to lie back, his hand slips beneath my hip, easing me up slightly before he flips me over onto my knees.

"God, yes," he says in a hungry voice, his hand sliding over my back, then palming my exposed ass. He smacks it gently and I let out a surprised gasp, which is replaced with a groan as he gently fingers my sensitive flesh with teasing flicks until I'm panting, wanting him again.

I feel him shift as he pushes his boxer briefs over his hips, feel his cock brush my entrance, but there is none of his usual tease, just a hard thrust.

I cry out, grabbing his pillow, nails digging into it as I bury my face. His hands are on my hips, his grip hard, perfect as he pounds inside me.

It's a delicious, harsh coupling unlike any we've had before, and it's exactly what I need. He *always* knows what I need.

His hand slides up my side, tangling in my hair and pulling my head back just slightly, with a roughness that creates a sharp stab of pleasure.

"Definitely not a nice girl," he growls softly, his hips never slowing their relentless pounding. "Come. Come with me *now.*"

My body arches as I sob my orgasm into the pillow, feeling the stiffening of his body behind me as my body milks his in perfect, simultaneous pleasure.

He pulls out and then collapses, nearly on top of me, his panting matching my own, as he curses and drops an arm over me, kissing my shoulder with a distracted gesture that seems more intuitive than deliberate.

As long as it's good, my mother had said, and I cling to it. I cling to it so hard, because right now, things are definitely, definitely good. So good that the thought of them ending makes my stomach knot up painfully.

I suck in a sharp breath of panic that sounds almost pained, and he lifts his head, looking at me in concern. His thumb touches my chin, studying my face. "Okay?"

Not okay. Not even a little bit okay.

My hands lift to his face, fingers tangling in his hair a little desperately. "Promise me," I say. "Promise me that this is all this is. Just sex. And that you're not going to pull a Thomas and turn it into some grand love story, that I'll inevitably turn into a tragedy."

"Mac—" Thomas swallows.

My fingers tighten. "Promise me you won't fall in love, and turn me into another Janie who has to break your heart."

His gaze goes from concerned to shuttered, and he dips his head in a single nod. "I promise."

My fingers relax.

The tension in my chest never does.

CHAPTER TWENTY-SIX

Friday, November 4

⌇

*I*t's customary for the groom's family to host the rehearsal dinner, and shocker, the Decker family likes itself some customary.

And lavish.

The night before Jon and Collette's wedding, they've rented out an entire rooftop bar with a view of the Empire State Building, custom cocktails, and a plated dinner so delicious that it should be outlawed on a night before most of us have to wear formalwear. I would kill for my comfiest sweatpants right now, if nothing else, to make more room for the lavish dessert table that's just been set up.

Across the room, Collette catches my eye and mimes me fetching her a plate, and I salute in confirmation. My best friend's sweet tooth preferences are as uncomplicated as sugar = good, so I set about getting her one of everything. Colorful macarons, dark, fudgy brownies, a blackberry cheesecake . . .

"No apple pie. A crime, wouldn't you agree?" I pivot and smile up at Thomas, looking painfully handsome in a light gray suit.

"Hey," I say, licking a bit of the blackberry sauce off my thumb, enjoying the way he tracks the motion.

"Don't," I say with a laugh. "I know that look."

"But I've barely seen you tonight," he grumbles, looking around to ensure nobody's paying us attention and then reaching for my hand. His thumb rubs circles against my palm that must have a direct line to my clit, because I nearly moan.

"Only because I'm not good at multi-tasking," I say, pulling my hand away before I lose my head. "Tonight and tomorrow, I'm maid of honor first and foremost. Then, I'm all yours."

It's true. I'm determined that Collette's wedding weekend goes off without a hitch, and I won't be able to do that as well if I'm constantly thinking about a quickie with Thomas.

Let me amend. I am constantly thinking about a quickie with Thomas, but thinking about it is different than acting on it.

However, it's not the whole truth.

I'm also uncomfortably aware of being in the presence of his entire family tonight, and tomorrow at the wedding as well.

I'll confess to being mildly curious about them, but wildly terrified. His other brother—the California start-up guy—seems harmless enough. A lot lanky, a little dorky, and quick to laugh.

His parents though—let's just say Mary and Dean Decker are everything I'd feared when I'd imagined Thomas's parents. They're both incredibly attractive, in the expensive, perfectly groomed kind of way. His father looks like he should be giving a speech in Congress or dashing in an ER to perform heart surgery on the president.

And Mary—ah yes, Mary. The Mary. The woman who has

inadvertently become an inside joke between Thomas and myself, a metaphorical ghost of our relationship.

But she's not a ghost tonight, she's here and she's Mary. She's a young sixty, if that, and looks better than most of the women here in a black sheath dress and really great heels. I'd sort of thought she'd have a "mom" haircut, a bob, or something, but her hair is just past her shoulders, thick and blonde, and if I had to guess from her toned calves, she's a runner like her son, or has a personal trainer.

I snort at the thought, because it was a personal trainer that actually brought Thomas and I together when Kris stood me up that fateful night.

"What's funny?" he asks, looking around the room.

"Nothing. This is a pretty great party. Your parents did an incredible job, especially considering they don't live in the city."

"My mom put in a lot of work," he says with no small amount of pride. "Apparently she chatted with Collette's wedding planner on a daily basis." He leans forward and whispers, "I think she might think this night is more important than the actual wedding."

I smile but I don't really feel it, because I'm too distracted by a thought that I never thought would make me as glum as it does:

Thomas hasn't introduced me. He hasn't even mentioned introducing me.

Collette hasn't either, but she's understandably busy. And I could introduce myself, of course, and under any other circumstances, I probably would, because I'm the maid of honor, and saying thank you for the party is the polite thing to do.

But these aren't just Jon's parents, not just the groom's parents, they're Thomas's parents.

And apparently he doesn't want me to meet them.

For that matter, he hasn't quite avoided me all night—we've both been busy—but it almost seems like he's waiting until everyone is busy and a few glasses of wine in before seeking me out.

What's that about?

"You going to eat all that?" Thomas asks, reaching for a peanut butter bar.

I smack his hand. "This is Collette's plate. And actually, would you mind taking this over to her? I have to use the ladies' room."

"Sure," he says, taking the plate, then gently grabbing my elbow with his other when I turn. "You okay?"

"Of course!" I smile, and his eyes narrow, but I pull away before he can study me in that way he has that sees straight to my soul.

It hadn't been a line. I really *do* have to use the bathroom. I'm adjusting my dress—a cute, strapless blue number—when I come out of the stall and come up short when I see a woman standing at the sinks, reapplying lipstick.

Of course. Of course it would be Thomas's mother. Apparently the universe seems determined to throw me in the path of all Deckers, not just Thomas.

"Hello there," Thomas's mother says, as she drops the lipstick back into her clutch and gives me a curious smile. "You're Mac, right? Collette's maid of honor?"

"Right, yes!" I say, stepping forward with a bright smile I usually reserve for meetings with my boss's bosses. "And you're the mother of the groom. I've been meaning to come over all night and tell you thank you so much for an amazing party."

White half-lie. No big.

"Is it?" She laughs and puts a hand to her stomach, as though nervous. "I've been in knots about it for months. Dean thinks I'm being ridiculous, that Jon and Collette would have been happy to celebrate with family in our backyard, but I wanted it to be special."

"Mission accomplished," I say, liking her more than I expected to. Up close there's a warmth about her that isn't immediately apparent from afar.

Not unlike her son . . .

"That said, I won't mind in the least if my other two sons want to wait a *decade* before marrying," she says, laughing. "All I've wanted for years is for them to settle down with a nice woman and make me grandbabies, but I'll need a breather after this!"

Do not pry, do not fish, do not . . .

"Hopefully they'll give you a bit of recovery time. Either of them close to the aisle?" I ask, oh-so-casually, as though simply making polite small talk as I wash my hands.

"My youngest definitely isn't. Aaron's always marched to the beat of his own drum, does things in his own way, in his own time. He told me when he was a boy he wasn't going to get married until he could do so on the moon, and I half think he probably still thinks that."

She smiles fondly.

"As for Thomas . . ."

I hold my breath, as she seems to give my question serious thought.

"I thought he'd be the first down the aisle. Both because he's the oldest, and the most traditional. Obviously Jon beat him to it, but let's just say I have a feeling he's not going to give me the long break in between mother-of-the-groom duties I'm hoping for.

And oh, gosh, as I say this, who am I kidding? I want so badly for him to find the right woman."

I feel so transparent, as though every emotion must be written all over my face: the pain of knowing I'm not the right woman, the discomfort with not being as forthright with Mary as she is with me.

"I'm sure he'll find her," I say, hoping she doesn't note the stiffness in my voice.

"You know, I think he already has," she says, lowering herself to a conspiratorial whisper.

I freeze, not sure if it's with hope or dread. Not sure what would be worse, her talking about me as future wifey, or some other woman. Thomas and I had agreed we weren't exclusive, he has been a little distant tonight. Maybe the wedding and his family's presence has nudged him back onto his original path, one that takes him away from Mac Austin.

"Yeah?" I force myself to ask. I have to know.

"I don't know for sure. Of all my boys, he wears his heart on his sleeve the least, but I also think he feels the deepest beneath all the reserve. And he mentioned a woman to me once, on the phone a couple of weeks ago—just once, but with maternal instincts, that's all it takes."

She winks at me, and I give another of those pasted-on smiles. "Does he not usually mention women to you?"

"Hmm? No, gosh no. Not since he had a bad breakup a while back. This is the first time I've heard his voice like this since then. Excited, a little . . . smitten, you know?"

I make a noncommittal noise, my ears buzzing.

"More than smitten perhaps." She is studying her reflection in the mirror, fluffing her hair with her hands, unaware of the furious butterflies in my stomach.

Me? Or someone else?

Both options feel equally terrifying.

"He even quit his job for this woman," Mary continues, with a laugh. "So I guess I'd better not be losing the wedding planner's number after all, huh?"

"What do you mean? Why would he do that?" The question is a little too sharp, and Mary looks at me in surprise, though her smile remains friendly.

She lifts her shoulders. "Apparently, this woman worked for him, and the company didn't allow for relationships with subordinates. He asked what he should do, and I told him it was relatively simple: he had to decide which was more important, the woman or the job. The next day, he called to tell me he'd quit."

Mary's gaze meets mine steadily in the mirror. "I guess he decided he wanted the woman more."

I'm not sure how I exited the bathroom. I know it wasn't with any sort of polite conversation, and my eyes are so blurred with tears that I practically mow down the person entering the bathroom as I try to exit.

Small hands that belong to someone as short as me find my elbows, steadying me. "Mac? Is everything okay?"

Reeling, I blink through the haze of tears, enough to make out the cute features of Stephanie Price, who swears softly when I stare mutely at her.

"Stupid question. You're so not okay," she says, maneuvering me through the crowd and out a side door onto the balcony with surprising strength.

It's brutally cold outside, cold even by November in New York standards, but I barely notice. I register it.

"Tell me what happened."

"I ran into Thomas's mom in the bathroom."

"Okay? First time meeting her?"

I nod. "Only she didn't know who I was, so she thought she was talking to a stranger about her other son's future nuptials, and . . ."

He quit his job for me. And I suspect, ended things with Anna because of me as well.

The realization is terrifying, because big gestures like that come from big emotions. Emotions such as . . .

My brain rejects even *thinking* the word.

And around the confusion, the panic, the sheer surprise, I feel something a little like anger bubble up.

He *promised* that it was just sex, that he wouldn't get his heart involved, so that I wouldn't have to *break* his heart . . .

I put a hand on my stomach and let out a gasp. "I hate him. I hate him for making me feel this way. I was just fine before he came along, I was just . . ."

I feel a sob coming on.

"Mac. I know it doesn't feel this way right now, but believe me when I say: you're going to be okay," Stephanie says soothingly.

I believe her. She's tiny but her voice is strong. And even though she's not wearing her combat boots tonight, her clunky Mary Janes look as though they'd double nicely as a weapon.

"This will work out as it's meant to, but in the mean time, what can I do?" she asks.

I manage a smile. "Be my bodyguard? I just . . . I can't deal with Thomas right now. I don't know what to say, or what to do . . ."

"No problem," she cuts in confidently. "I can run interference, and even enlist Ethan to help as well, but on one condition," Stephanie says, raising a finger to get my attention.

"What?"

"I'll help you stall this conversation with him, but that's all it'll be. A delay. You have to promise me that you *will* have the conversation. Just as soon as you possibly can without affecting Collette's day."

I take a deep breath. It's brutal, but she's right. The sooner we have the conversation, the sooner we can move on.

My conversation with my mom replays in my head. *At the end of the day, it's the kindest thing we can do for someone else—letting them go before things turn ugly.*

I missed the turn; they've *already* gotten a little ugly, because I'm faced with a realization that makes me ache inside:

I'm either going to have to risk my heart . . . or break Thomas's.

And I just don't think I'm brave enough for the first one.

CHAPTER TWENTY-SEVEN

Saturday, November 5

～

$\mathcal{M}$y plan was *almost* pretty good. I made it through the rest of the rehearsal dinner without having to talk to Thomas with relative ease.

He'd been preoccupied by conversation with his family, many of whom were from out of town for the wedding. And any time he made his way towards me, I'd chat up someone else. The closest call had been when I was on my way out, waiting for my coat at coat check, and Thomas had made his way over with a dark frown.

Stephanie's husband is a peach. Ethan Price had stepped into Thomas's path, giving me the chance to head home.

Thomas must have gotten the hint, because he'd texted only once. **You okay?**

No. Not okay.

I'd replied that I had a headache, even adding the headache emoji for good measure. It's the oldest, lamest line in the book, but it's a classic for a reason. It worked. He told me to feel better, drink lots of water, and that he'd see me tomorrow.

And so here I am.

Tomorrow is today, and I feel less up to facing him than ever.

The morning had been easy enough. Maid of honor duties had kept me plenty busy and out of his path. Bow tying, hair curling, safety-pin hunting, bouquet distributing . . .

It had all been perfectly diverting, right up until the moment I didn't think through, and thus didn't plan for.

For all its hastiness, Collette and Jon's wedding is classic to the max, which means we follow every tradition to the letter. Right down to the maid of honor preceding Collette and her dad down the aisle.

By myself. Walking towards Jon. And his best man.

Thomas.

My smile never wavers, of that I'm very sure, because it feels frozen in place. I try to keep my attention on the pleasant-looking pastor. An over-the-moon happy Jon. Collette's mom, who's already crying.

But like a damned beacon those silver eyes call to me, I feel them, I feel him, and in a moment of weakness, just steps away from the altar of the church, my eyes flick his way, my gaze colliding with him.

My breath whooshes out, softly, and I feel something more terrifying than yesterday's anger.

A little click of possibility for something I never, ever even thought about. The possibility of some day walking down this aisle, on my mom's arm, finding those same silver eyes waiting for me, with Jon there too, but the two men would be in reverse order . . .

Only my love, loyalty and genuine happiness for Collette gets me through the next few moments, and I redirect my tidal wave of emotions towards *her*, telling myself that the tears that won't stop leaking from my eyes are only happiness for my friend, and not mourning for me.

I make it through the ceremony and dinner unscathed, thanks to some helpful interference from Stephanie, but even she can't help me come toast-time. Thomas is best man to my maid of honor, which means we stand beside each other, and I half expect him to corner me and ask what's going on—he knows, I know he knows something is up.

But he betrays nothing, not even when I finish my speech (I crushed it), and our fingers brush while exchanging the microphone for his speech, which he also crushes, although in a more cerebral way than my joke-filled speech.

Then the dancing starts, and at the first slow song, my reprieve is over. Thomas doesn't ask me to dance, so much as demands it with his eyes as he makes his way towards me.

Stephanie tries to step into his path, but he cuts her with a searing gaze, and she takes a startled step back. She tries to step forward once more, but her husband touches her arm, shakes his head *no*.

Traitor. Ethan Price is clearly on Thomas's side and thus dead to me.

Thomas stops in front of me, extends a hand. Not a word, just a single palm. There are a million excuses I could make and yet, I find myself putting my hand in his, letting him lead me to the dance floor.

In spite of my mood, I relax for the first time in twenty-four hours when I step into his arms. It's that same baffling contradiction again, that the same man who causes all of my confusion and frustration is also the one to soothe it.

Everything about him is sure and steady. His shoulder against my cheek. His hand holding mine. His arm holding me so close.

He shifts the grip of his right hand slightly, and for a second I realize he wants to let go, but it's only to reposition, maneuvering the long strand of blue hair that Collette had wanted me to pull out of the updo "for flair," and wrapping it once around his finger.

I want to weep.

"Thomas," I manage on a whisper.

"No," he says quietly, firmly. "No. Not here, not now. You're going to end things between us, and I'm going to let you, because that was our deal. But first, Mac, you'll give me this dance. *This* will be what you remember when you think of us, not the conversation we'll have when it's over, and not whatever's caused that conversation. And even if it's not what you remember, let it be what I remember. Please."

I close my eyes, and unlike at the ceremony, when the tears come this time, there's no pretending it's due to wedding happiness.

The song is one of Collette's favorites, that cheesy-yet-classic Aerosmith song, "I Don't Want to Miss a Thing," and though I know every word, I haven't actually really listened to the words until now, and they're an achingly perfect fit for Thomas's request to let us have this moment, this dance. The perfect song for us, being present now, not missing a thing because it can be gone at any minute.

"How'd you know?" I whisper. "That I was ending things."

He inhales slowly, his hand moving up slightly on my back,

fingers pressing against the fabric of my dress, as though to keep me close. Closer. "I just know. I always know, with you."

Don't let me go.

But I know that he will, if I ask him to. And I *am* going to ask him to, because if I've learned anything in all this, it's that I want Thomas Decker to be happy. And if that means letting him go, to find the future wife I can never be, I never want to be . . . then I'll let *him* go.

No matter how much it hurts.

CHAPTER TWENTY-EIGHT

Saturday, November 5

⁓

*J*on and Collette's reception is in the ballroom of a fancy, old-school hotel on the Upper East Side, with Central Park just across the street.

When the song ends, Thomas takes my hand and leads me to the coat check. No words are exchanged, not until we find ourselves on a bench just inside the entrance of Central Park.

"Alright," he says, after we wait for a giggling teenage couple to go by. "I had my dance. Now you get your say."

I look down at my feet, my fancy pink stilettos that match my fancy bridesmaid dress. I take a minute, gather my thoughts.

"You quit your job for me," I say.

His head whips around. For all his talk about knowing me, he hadn't seen that coming, and he lets out a low groan.

"Yeah." I smile a little. "Mary told me. I finally met your mother, and she dropped a *bit* of a bombshell."

Thomas turns towards me. "Mac—"

"No, you said I get my say," I say hurriedly, so I can get this out.

"I wish you wouldn't have done that; quit for me. Or maybe I just wish I'd never learned about it, because now that I know . . ."

I turn to face him too, our knees bumping, his gaze level, if a bit pained.

"You've been managing this whole thing since the very beginning, haven't you? I was the project, and you had a plan from the beginning. Everything that I thought was spontaneous, everything I thought was us 'winging it,' even your speech about how we could take this one day at a time, and that we don't have to be exclusive, that we don't have to put a label on it. That was crafted so that I wouldn't freak out, wasn't it? You were just corralling me into the relationship you wanted, but doing it so silly, under disguise, that I wouldn't know until I was trapped in it, right?"

He closes his eyes. "When you put it that way, it sounds so manipulative."

"Alright." I keep my voice light, because I truly don't want to hurt him. "Put it in a different way."

He opens his eyes. "I never wanted to trap you, Mac. Never. But did I hope that someday, you'd . . ." He blows out a breath. "For what it's worth, I didn't start out with a *plan*, as you put it. That night on your couch, I wanted to kiss you. I wanted to do a hell of a lot more than kiss you. But there was Anna, who I was sort of seeing, and I'm not a cheater, I'll never be a cheater. And then there was the job thing. And . . . do I at least get a little credit for acting out of character?" He smiles. "I mean, I quit my job because I wanted to kiss a woman. It's the most un-me thing I've ever done."

It's a little romantic. A lot romantic. *I don't want romance.*

"Why didn't you just tell me that? So I could make my own decisions."

"I meant to! It was the plan. That day I was outside the office we shared. I couldn't come in, because I didn't have a security badge, and I had this . . ." He laughs, and rubs a hand over his face. "I was going to kiss you right there in the street, romantic-comedy style. But I'm not good with emotions, or . . . any of it, and before I could get the words out, you were going on about rekindling things with Crotch V."

It's my turn to groan.

"So, I'm standing there," he continues, "and I don't know, I guess I just felt furious. I'd given up a job I didn't want, and that didn't matter so much, but I'd lost my chance with the woman I did want, and . . . I was pissed, Mac."

He laughs, quietly. "I was so pissed. At myself, at you, definitely at V-Cut. When Jon asked if I could give you a ride to Vermont, I said yes because he's my brother, and it was his weekend, but I didn't want to. I didn't want anything to do with you, you turned my life upside down. You have done from that very first day at the bar, and I was over it, over you . . ."

I pull my coat a little closer around my chin and look down at the ground again.

"But you're everywhere, Mac. Not just everywhere I turn, though that's been true, but you got everywhere *here*." He puts his hand on his chest. "And no matter how hard I tried to tell myself that I could let you go when you wanted, I also knew that I'd hate myself if I didn't at least *try* to make you feel what I felt."

The space that follows his statement feels huge and empty and massive, and I know—I know that if I asked him what he felt, he'd tell me, just like I know that when he tells me, I'll crack under the pressure of not knowing what to do with it.

Of knowing I'll hurt him.

"My mom told me that the kindest thing we can do for someone is to let them go before things turn ugly," I say, forcing myself to meet his eyes. "This is me, doing that. We can't afford to explode, Thomas. *Implode*, maybe. But this can't go down in a fiery 'go to hell' shitstorm. Collette is like a sister to me, and Jon is your brother. Even if we weren't always going to be a part of each other's lives through them, there's that whole fated-to-bump-into-each-other thing."

"You don't think that means something?" he asks, his voice urgent now. Hurting. He takes my hand. "You don't think the fact that my face popped up on your dating app *when I was sitting next to you* meant something? Or that I happened to take a job at your company that very same week meant something? Or that your best friend was marrying my brother?"

"I think maybe it meant that Fate has a funny sense of humor," I say. "But let's not forget, when we saw each other on that dating app, neither was interested. That means something too, Thomas. That we aren't meant for each other."

He looks away, and I squeeze his hand, begging him to understand.

"I believe in first impressions. Gut feelings. Intuition. You don't want the girl with blue hair, Thomas."

He opens his mouth, but I set my hand lightly over his lips, stopping the words. "You think you do now. I'm a novelty. You've been one to me too. But it's time for us to get on with our real lives."

His gray eyes do something I haven't seen before, something shiny and terrible, and I shake my head even as my own eyes do the shiny thing too.

"No," I say vehemently. "You said. You said that if I want to walk away, at any point, I could. You said I wouldn't have to give a breakup speech, though this sort of feels like one.

"And you said," I continue on a breath. "That there'd be no fear of hurting you, no pressure to stay longer than I want to."

"Because you aren't supposed to want to walk away, Mac," he says, angry now, though he takes a deep breath, as though trying to regain control.

His eyes are miserable. "I'll let you go. I said I would, and I will, but won't you just tell me why? What I did? It can't be because I quit my job for you. That's not it."

"No," I agree. "No, that wasn't it."

I mean to say *anything* else, but I don't, and Thomas watches me with a patient, resigned look on his face.

Finally, he sighs. "You don't *know* why, do you? You have no idea why you're walking away from me."

Wordlessly, I shake my head, tears running down my cheeks.

He nods. "Okay. Okay." Then he pulls me close, kisses the top of my head, and pulls me against his side, his arm wrapped around me as I cry.

It's not a breakup speech.

But it *is* a goodbye.

CHAPTER TWENTY-NINE

Friday, November 11

~

*S*ince I don't really do relationships, I don't do breakups either. But I have had some nasty parting of ways with some of my flings, and normally it's Collette who gets me through them, armed with ice cream and action movies, and *guys are the worst*.

Jon and Collette are honeymooning in Iceland, and I'm not so pathetic that I'd crash that with my melancholy, so I find myself leaning on another friend instead, a new one, but the only person who has a semblance of understanding of my situation.

"Damn," Stephanie says, after I've repeated the entire story for the second time at her direction. "Damn, he is . . ."

I narrow my eyes. "Don't even think about saying something like 'pretty great.'"

He's not pretty great. He's really great. I know it and I don't want to hear it.

Stephanie holds up her hands innocently. "Okay, okay. But can I ask something that has to do with you? Nothing to do with Thomas?"

"Sure." I wipe my nose.

"When you were a little girl. Like, nine," Stephanie says, pouring a bit more whisky in my glass, then her own. "What was your favorite fairy tale? Like, were you into the super-dark ones? The Disney versions? Write your own, so the princess saved the prince?"

I shake my head. "None of the above. We didn't have a TV. My mom wasn't really the 'read before bed' type. I wasn't a read at all type. I knew they existed, of course, but only in sort of the loose concept."

"I see. So you never imagined your Prince Charming?"

"Definitely not." I grab a handful of Goldfish.

"Okay. And what about romantic comedies? Hallmark Christmas movies? Romance novels?"

I shake my head. "Not a fan. I like my movies with lots of explosions. My favorite book genre is true crime. The only Christmas movie I like is *Die Hard*, and maybe *The Grinch*."

"And your mom—you said she never married? What about your dad?"

I shrug. "He wasn't in the picture. My mom told him she was pregnant, he wasn't interested, so I'm not interested. And no, Mom never married. Not even close."

"Okay," Stephanie says, nodding. "Okay. I'm going to give you some homework. Now first, I'm going to put up the disclaimer that as a modern woman, I don't think every woman needs a man. I don't think every couple needs a piece of paper in order to have a healthy, happy relationship. But I would like to offer up some, shall we say, counter examples to your way of thinking."

"Alright," I say, more curious than anything else.

She gets out her phone. "I'm going to text you a movie list. I want you to watch all of them. You don't have to like them, just watch them."

My phone buzzes, and I pick it up to see the message she's just sent. I'm not surprised to see that it's a list of romantic comedies and fairy tales, but neither am I excited.

"Really?" I say.

She merely smiles. "Think of it as food for thought. You can even rage against them if you want, I've done plenty of that. But watch them. Oh, and one extra little part of the assignment."

"What?" I'm fully wary now.

Stephanie touches my arm lightly. "Invite your mom over. Have her watch them with you."

CHAPTER THIRTY

Sunday, November 27

⌒

"*Well?*" I ask, turning off the TV and rolling my head on the couch cushion to look at my mom, sprawled on the other side. "What did you think?"

A dreamy smile crosses her face. "I quite liked that last one. A British dork and a movie star. Who would have thought?"

"No one," I say. "Because it's make-believe. Show me Hugh Grant's and Julia Roberts' characters five years after the movie ends. I'm betting they're divorced."

The words feel automatically preprogrammed in me, but honestly? I don't feel the words like I used to.

Because I too liked the movie. I've liked all of the movies.

Stephanie knew what she was doing.

Mom gives me a fond smile, looking a little thoughtful. "Have you spoken to Thomas?"

I give her a glare, because I've told her at least ten times tonight that *he* is not open for discussion. And even if he were, the discussion has been short.

Have you spoken to Thomas?

Nope.

See? End of conversation.

"Okay, okay," she relents. "How's the new job going?"

I narrow my eyes, skeptical of the change in subject, but she seems interested, for once. "Really great, actually. It's a challenge, and I feel over my head at times, but I'm surprised by how much I like having something to sink my teeth into, and something where I can set up long-term vision rather than just checking off the next immediate task."

"I'm really glad. And really proud."

I take a deep breath and look at her through one squinted eye, braced. "Is this the part where you ask me for money to fund your physical therapy schooling?"

She winces and sits upright, reaching for her water glass. "I deserve that. I do. But no, I'm done with that. I've decided to take a cue from my brilliant daughter and try to be a grown-up. I've buckled down at the salon a bit more. Encouraged my clients to book out a month in advance rather than telling them I could maybe squeeze them in if I didn't get a better invitation to Atlantic City."

"Wow." *Wow.* "That's great. Right?"

"It is," she says slowly. "It's not my dream job or anything, but I think I could use a little practice at discipline."

"Who are you? What have you done with my mother?"

Her smile is distracted, almost mysterious. She nods towards the TV. "Let's play the next one on Steph's list."

"The last one? Let's do it."

She looks disappointed. "That's all we have? But we've been having so much fun these past few weekends."

Per Stephanie's suggestion, I invited my mom for the movie viewing session. Every Sunday night we've watched two or three of the movies until we've made it all the way through.

"Well, that's too bad," Mom says, standing and folding the blanket. Even that is a first.

"Mom, is everything okay?" I ask, a little nervously. "You didn't get a call from the doctor, right? No diagnosis you want to tell me about . . ."

She laughs. "Dear God, Mac, what have I done to you that you think me being in love resembles me dying."

My eyes widen. "In *love*?"

"His name is Richard, and he's very sweet."

I don't respond. I don't think I've ever heard my mom even use the L word in relation to a man before. Or describe a man as sweet.

"Of course, the old fart is ridiculously old-fashioned," Mom says, rolling her eyes. "We've been on five dates now, and he still won't let me get in his pants."

The surprises just keep coming. "You haven't slept together?"

"Not yet. We're just sort of enjoying each other. Not like some of these movies," she says, pointing at the screen and smiling a little fondly.

"You're being courted by a guy named Richard. Who you're not sleeping with. All because my friend made us watch *The Little Mermaid*?" I ask skeptically.

"I think your friend is very wise." She pats my leg.

"You do?" I don't think I've ever been this thrown off in a conversation with my mom. "What happened to letting things go before they turned sour, and living in the moment, and oh, I don't know, everything else you've been preaching at me for decades?"

She turns uncharacteristically serious. Even a little sad. "It's possible I could be wrong about some things. It happens. What about you, baby girl? Ever been wrong about some things?"

I cross my arms. "I know what you're getting at. *Who* you're getting at. And it's going to take more than a few ancient Meg Ryan movies to convince me that Thomas and I will be anything other than incompatible opposites."

"Ancient!" She places a hand on her chest. "Ouch! Fair enough, but if not Thomas, then at least get yourself a rebound."

There. That sounds a bit more like my mother. I relax slightly.

"What about that dating app that you always said turned up some pretty great hotties?" she says.

"Well, *hotties* is your word," I say. "But TapThat? Hmm. I haven't been on in . . . a while."

"Before Thomas" is what I mean to say and don't, and my mom must sense it because she sighs and picks up my phone, handing it to me.

"I'm going to try my hand at some tough love, Mackenzie Rochelle Austin: Put on your big girl pants and get the hell back out there."

CHAPTER THIRTY-ONE

Thursday, December 1

⌖

I don't get back on TapThat.

I think about it—not just because of my mom's pep talk, but because I really do want a cure for this malaise that's not like anything I've experienced before.

I'm okay at work. I love the new job, and luckily, my team seems to love me in the new job too, which is more important than my bosses approving (though they seem pleased as well, go me!).

But while work should be a total distraction from missing Thomas, it also makes me think of him. Whenever something good or annoying happens, my first inclination is to text him. And whether I leave the remote office (I'm still doing final touches on C&S) or the main office, my feet always seem to want to turn in the direction of his place rather than home.

Because he feels like home.

The weekends are even worse. I still say yes to brunch invitations, still put on my pushup bra and heels when I get a tipsy text message from Sadie at 11pm on Saturday to come dancing. And I still have fun, but I also find myself wanting just a bit more.

Someone to share it all with.

And let's face it, the advice to get back out there came from my *mom*. Based on her track record, it's probable that she and this Richard will fizzle out by tomorrow, and she'll resume her semi-regular booty calls with the bouncer at a strip club named Donko.

Mostly though, I haven't bothered to get on the app, because I'm stalling. I'm stalling having to talk to someone who isn't Thomas, to kiss someone who doesn't have his gray eyes. I need more time to get him out of my system, and since it's the first time I've ever had to do that with a guy, I'm trying to be patient with myself.

However, my time's run out. My mom wants me to meet Richard and her for dinner this weekend, and it's "highly suggested" that I bring a date.

I could ignore the suggestion, obviously, but I'm also choosing to use this as the kick in the butt I need to get back out there. I used to recruit guys to be my plus-one like it was nobody's business. It's time to put old Mac back into circulation.

I pull a beer out of the fridge and open TapThat.

The first three guys are hard nos. One is wearing some sort of weird handkerchief situation. The other has a tattoo on half his face that I think is a scorpion? I love tattoos, but this guy has mugshot vibes.

The third dude is, I think, doing an Elvis impression?

The fourth is a no as well. He looks like he'd have bad breath.

The fifth, no. He's not smiling, and not in the sexy way, but the mugshot way.

I almost tap yes on number eight, but he reminds me a tiny bit too much of Thomas, only he isn't Thomas.

God. I take a swig of beer and look at the ceiling. This isn't working.

I take another drink and eye the *Surprise Me!* button at the bottom of the app.

It's a relatively new feature of the app that I haven't used yet. It displays your matches, not with their face but by location. It brings up a map of your area, and displays green dots for any potential matches that are "out on the town" and looking to meet up.

A digital booty call, basically, except the app uses your GPS location, only showing you what the other person looks like when you arrive at the actual location. It's the ultimate wild card, straddling the line between exciting and nuts, and leaning towards the latter.

Isn't that what you wanted? a little devil on my shoulder nudges. To be the type of person who jumps in with both feet, eyes closed, and then is able to get back out just as easily?

Yes. Yes it is, little devil.

I feel almost desperate to connect with that part of myself, that part I think might be dying, and so I tap the Surprise Me button, then hit the only green light that's even remotely in my neighborhood. Apparently six pm on a Thursday is not exactly a hot zone of Manhattan dating.

I hold my breath, waiting for the app to confirm that the other person's agreed to stay where they are and meet me, and when it comes through affirmatively, I'm not sure I'm elated or dismayed.

I don't have time to be either, because then I read the smaller font:

Your date will expect you in 10–15 minutes.

Eek! I glance at the location. It'll take me just under ten to get there, which gives me almost no time at all to get pretty.

My work outfit today is pretty boring by my standards – black boots, jeans, and a black turtleneck – but I sort of love the way it looks with my current hairstyle hair, which is now . . .

Wait for it . . .

Rainbow!

Or rather, platinum on top, with the last few inches or so a pastel cupcake-esque rainbow. My favorite part about it is that I can pull my hair back in a low bun, and from the front, I look like a regular blonde, but then the back is a literal swirl of color.

I decide to go full unicorn mode for the date, pulling it over my shoulders and giving the rainbow parts a quick scrunch for some body. Might as well let the poor guy know what he's dealing with upfront.

I have time to brush my teeth, add a swipe of lipgloss, and grab my purse. I speed-walk, so as not to be late. Normally, timeliness doesn't stress me out, but I don't want a stranger to think I've stood him up; after all, being stood up is how I landed myself in this whole mess in the first place.

I'm so focused on getting there on time that I don't realize until I get to the marked intersection that this isn't just any old bar.

This is *the* bar. Smoke & Baron, the place I met Thomas. Well, where I *first* met him.

"You've got to be shitting me," I mutter.

It takes all of my courage to open the door and go inside, and I do so only by telling myself that the only way to close a door is to open a door, or some nonsense BS pep talk like that.

My phone buzzes. TapThat, confirming my arrival with the photo of the guy I'm looking for. I tap, and then stop in my tracks when I see the man I'm meeting.

He's not at all someone I would have tapped yes on. He's too clean-cut, too preppy, too . . .

Thomas.

He's Thomas.

Mine. My Thomas.

My love.

I get now why Stephanie made me watch those movies. It's so I understood the importance of the all-important ending scene. So that I would know my moment, my scene.

And this is it.

Slowly, I lift my eyes to the familiar shoulders, the blue suit. I wait for the urge to flee, but interestingly, it never comes. It never even flickers.

My heart is in my throat as I walk to the bar, the heels of my boots clicking softly until I'm beside him. Without a word, I sit on the stool beside him, placing my phone, screen up on the bar, just close enough for him to see.

Thomas glances at my phone where his picture is still on the screen. "Hard pass on that guy, huh?"

I let out a laugh. "Oh, I don't know. He's not so bad."

His eyes lift to mine, but instead of the gladness I'm hoping for, I see wariness. So wary it makes my chest ache. I've *hurt* him. I can see that I have, and yet he's here, and he must have tapped the green light, seen my face on the app, because he isn't surprised it's me.

And yet he didn't leave. Hope flares, tiny but bright. I cling to it.

The bartender—the same woman as before—sets a napkin in

front of me, and the curious way she looks between us makes me wonder if she remembers us.

"Malbec?" she asks me.

Yup. She remembers alright. I smile. "Please."

"How have you been?" I ask Thomas quietly, after she's placed my drink in front of me.

"Fine. Good."

"The freelance thing? Going well?"

He nods. "Very. I already have more work than I can handle, I'm thinking about bringing on a couple of guys I used to work with. Maybe starting a small consulting firm. I like the hair, by the way."

"Yeah, thanks, and hey, congrats about the job thing!" I tap his arm, trying for casual. His eyes fix on my fingers resting on his suit jacket, and I pull them back.

"And Elodie?" he says. "How'd the C&S launch go?"

"Just wrapping up! I think it'll be great. Everything else is . . . great. Overall, I'm just super happy."

Ugh, why do I sound so lame? Why is this so awkward?

Oh yeah, Mac, because you basically crapped all over this guy's heart.

"I'm glad." He looks at his drink, "Look, Mac, this was a mistake—"

"I'm not really happy," I blurt out. "I mean, yeah, work is great, but I'm not *happy* happy. Not like I was when I was with you."

"With me."

"When we were together," I say, a little bit pleading.

His eyebrows go up, his expression still cool. "Were we together? I wasn't aware we were allowed to apply labels to it."

I flinch. "That's fair. That's fair."

"Look." He stares at his drink then back at me. "I care about you. I want the best for you. I hope that some day we can be friends. But you ripped my heart out that night, Mac. I know that's not fair. I told you that you could leave without hurting me, but I lied. It *did* hurt, and you were right. You were right in that our wants are incompatible. You want fun and temporary, and I want . . . I want forever, Mac. I want that with someone."

A lump forms in my throat at his words, even though I know I've earned every bit of Thomas's censure and then some.

"Someone," I repeat softly. *Not me.*

"I actually had someone specific in mind," he smiles ruefully, staring down at his drink. "This blue-haired girl. But she wasn't interested."

The light of hope that was nearly extinguished flickers a tiny bit brighter.

"She sounds like a complete idiot," I say with feeling. "What if . . ." I swallow nervously. "What if there was a rainbow-haired girl who was a lot like the blue-haired girl, but much smarter. This rainbow-haired girl, she . . . understands now, the only thing more terrible than forever with the wrong person . . ."

I wait until he meets my eyes to finish. "Would be forever without you."

Thomas doesn't move. Doesn't say a word, and I feel like my heart could break even as I know I deserve it. I had my chance, and I blew it.

"Mac—" he says finally.

"I love you, Thomas," I whisper, and his head whips towards mine.

I force myself to hold his searching, stunned gaze.

The words still feel funny on my tongue—I don't know that I've ever said them, even to people I do love like my mom and Collette. I've certainly never said them to a man, and he must know it, because his face crumples softly in understanding.

"Mac." This time it's a whisper. And he touches my face.

"Am I doing this wrong? Is this not how it's done?" I ask, feeling completely raw and vulnerable. "Was I not supposed to say I love you—"

His mouth covers mine, lips coaxing mine open as he tilts my head slightly to deepen a kiss that has way more tongue than in the movies.

"You were *definitely* supposed to say it," he says roughly, when he pulls back. "Hell, Mac, I wouldn't have minded if you said it a long time ago, say right around the time when I fell in love with you."

My heart leaps, and my smile widens with all the happiness bursting out of me. "And when was that?"

He merely smiles and pulls me in for another kiss, but I set a finger over his mouth at the last moment. "Wait. What are you doing here?"

Thomas gives a joking sigh. "So your bout with romantic talk. That was just a one-time thing?"

"No, I mean, on the app." I press a nail to my phone. "I rejected you weeks ago. And you me. We shouldn't have been matched again."

"Ah. That." He grins. "Let's just say we had a little help from an unlikely source."

"Who?" I demand.

"Your mom. She got my number from Collette, and sent me a *very* heavily emojied text message telling me to delete my TapThat account and start a new one."

"But—*why?*" Even for my mom, that's out there.

"I believe she wanted us to have another chance," Thomas says softly, picking up the ends of my rainbow hair, and studying them.

"Huh. It was a long shot," I say, shaking my head.

"Was it? Or maybe she just knew." He reaches out and hooks a hand on the bottom of my bar stool, tugging me closer.

"Knew what?"

"The universe was really never going to settle for us not being together." Thomas kisses my cheek, my chin. My lips. Then smiles. "Don't go skeptical on me. You're the one that said we've been thrown together in three different ways in a single week, and now this one. Though this one's different."

"How so?" I manage in between kisses.

"Because this time, darling Mac, I'm not letting you go."

Epilogue

I'm true to my word. I don't let her go.

Oh, I'm patient. I'm nothing if not patient. I let the love of my life thrive and grow and get promoted at Elodie again. I let her drag me out dancing at two in the morning, and learn to scuba dive, and hold her hand while she gets a tattoo of a bee on her butt, for no other reason than it was on the page she flipped open to in the tattoo parlor.

I don't let go, but I don't ask, either. Not until she's ready. Not until I know she'll say yes.

And then she does, and I'm the happiest man alive.

The destination wedding is intimate and casual, at a very special little bed and breakfast in Vermont. The bridal party is small: my brothers with me, Stephanie and Collette with Mac. My family is there, of course, and her mom, with Richard who she keeps vowing to make an honest man out of.

The cake? We skipped it. Did apple pie instead.

Throughout the entire engagement, Mac threatened to wear

black on our wedding day, and I rolled with it. She can wear whatever color she wants, just so long as her end destination is me. So, I'm ready for black. Green. Rainbow.

I'm not, however, ready for her choice of a fluffy white ballroom dress, nor am I ready for the tears in my eyes when I see her.

The only surprise bigger than Mac's traditional dress choice is the fact that Mary and Annette have become close friends. My mother paid the down payment for Mac's mom to open her own salon. Mac's mom has already paid her back and made my mother her first client.

And speaking of hair, Mac brought back her blue streak for me as a wedding gift—her something blue.

My gift to her? A confession I've been holding on to for over a year.

I never tapped "no" on Mac on that dating app. She was a hell yes for me. Always has been.

Keep an eye out for more
sparkling rom-coms
coming soon from

LAUREN LAYNE

HEADLINE
ETERNAL

Made in Manhattan

A dazzling opposites-attract rom-com
from Lauren Layne!

**Sometimes the best things come
from unexpected places . . .**

Available now from

Online chemistry is nothing compared
to offline rivalry in this sparkling
enemies-to-lovers rom-com!

Available now from

The Prenup

Don't miss Lauren Layne's hilarious and
romantic standalone novel

**This match made in practicality is about
to take on whole new meaning . . .**

Available now from

HEADLINE
ETERNAL

They vowed to steer clear of Manhattan's heartbreakers – but when it comes to love, some risks are worth taking . . .

Lauren Layne's *The Central Park Pact* series is available now!

Meet *The Wedding Belles.*
They can make any bride's dream come true.
And now it's their turn.

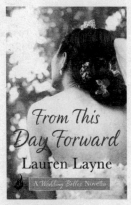

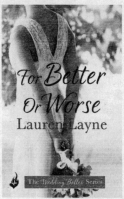

Available now from

**Love comes unexpectedly in these
sexy standalones from Lauren Layne!**

Available from